A COLORING BOOK

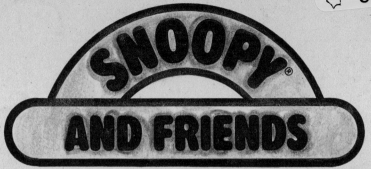

SNOOPY®
AND FRIENDS

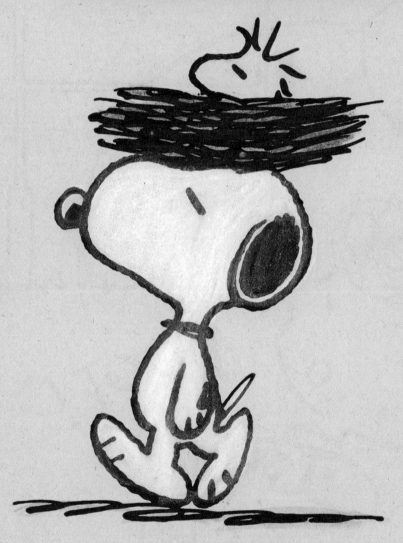

GOLDEN® and GOLDEN & DESIGN®
are trademarks of Western Publishing Company, Inc.

A GOLDEN® BOOK
Western Publishing Company, Inc.
Racine, Wisconsin 53404

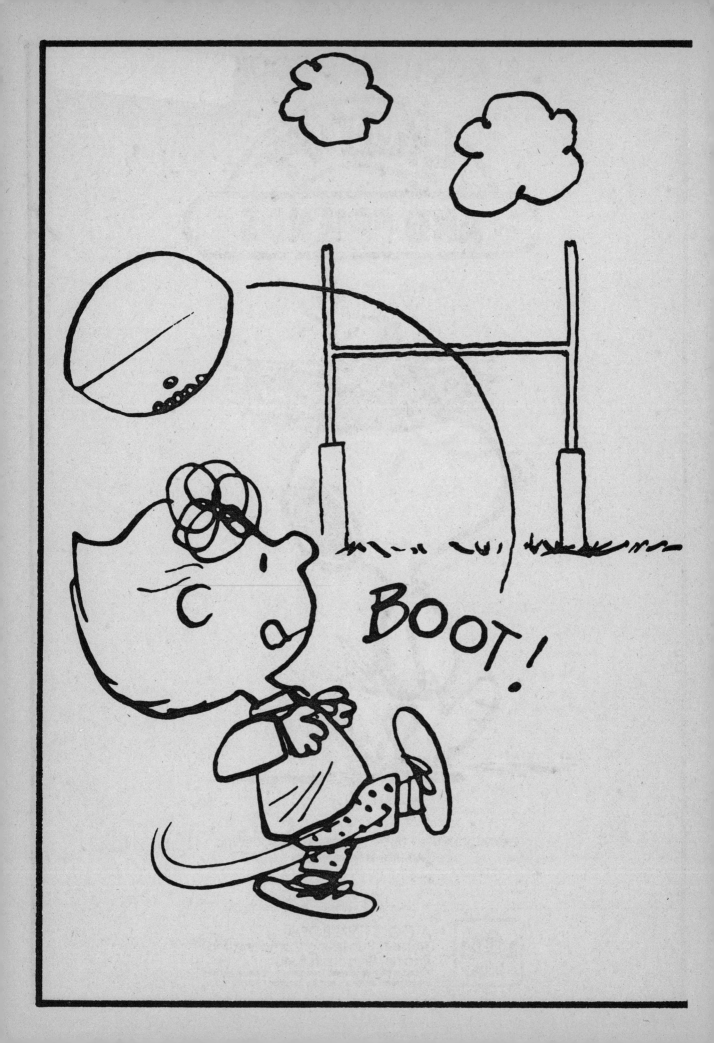

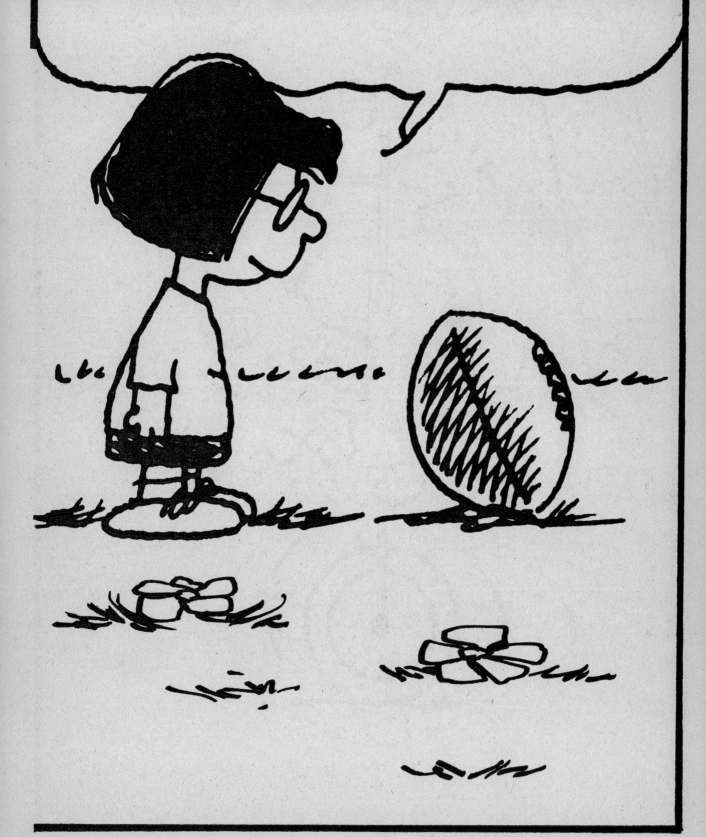

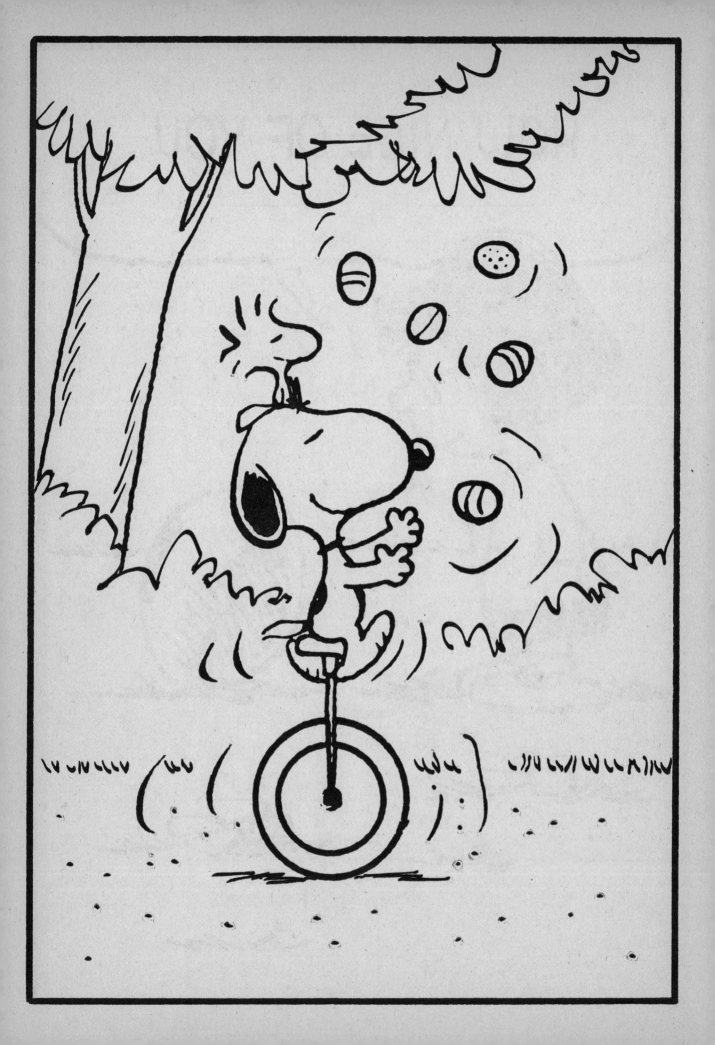

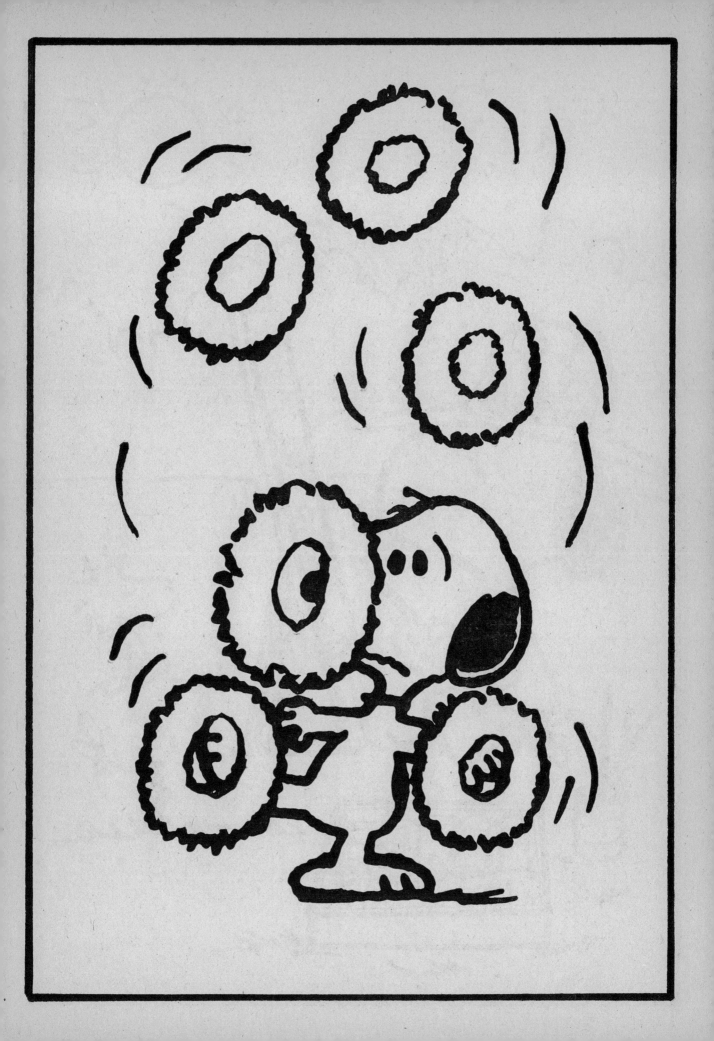

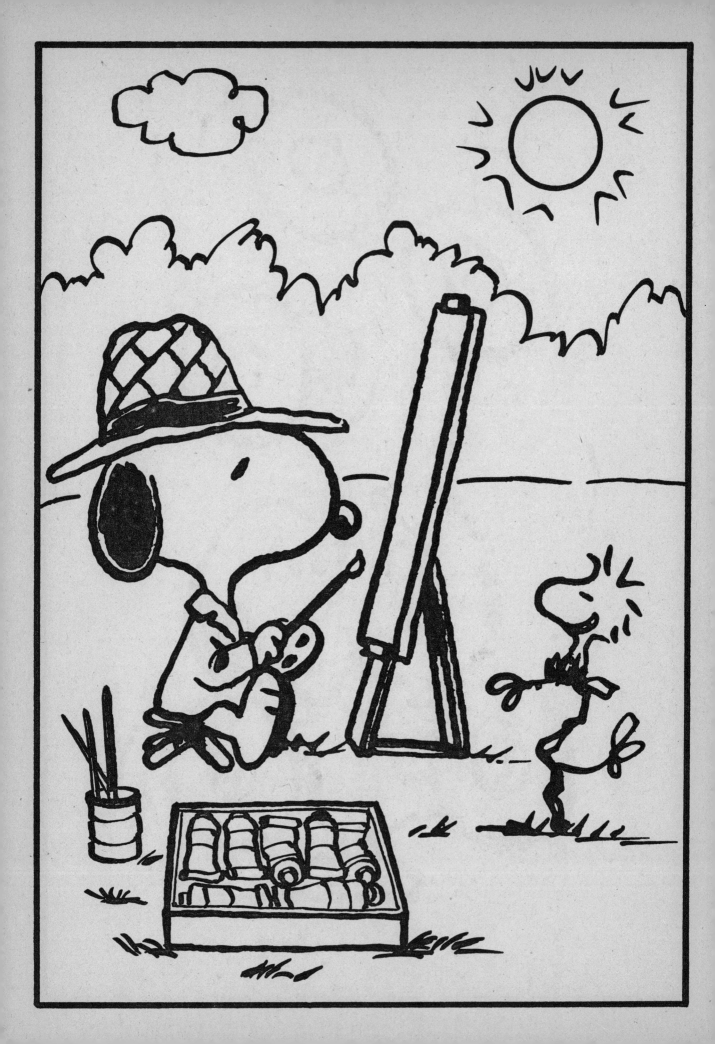

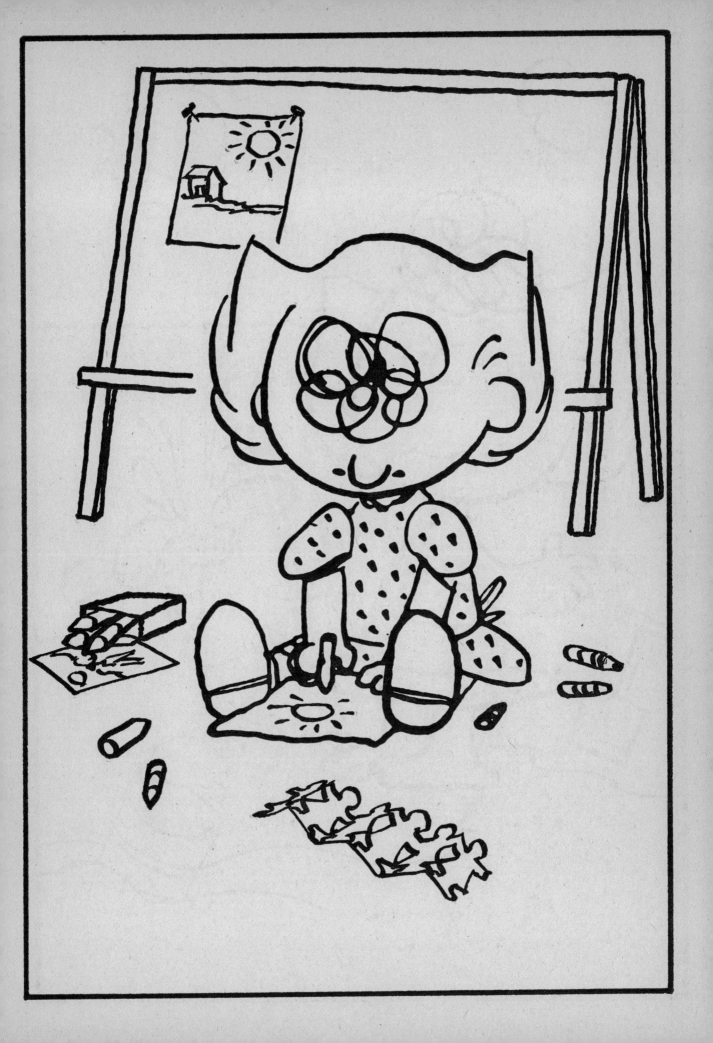

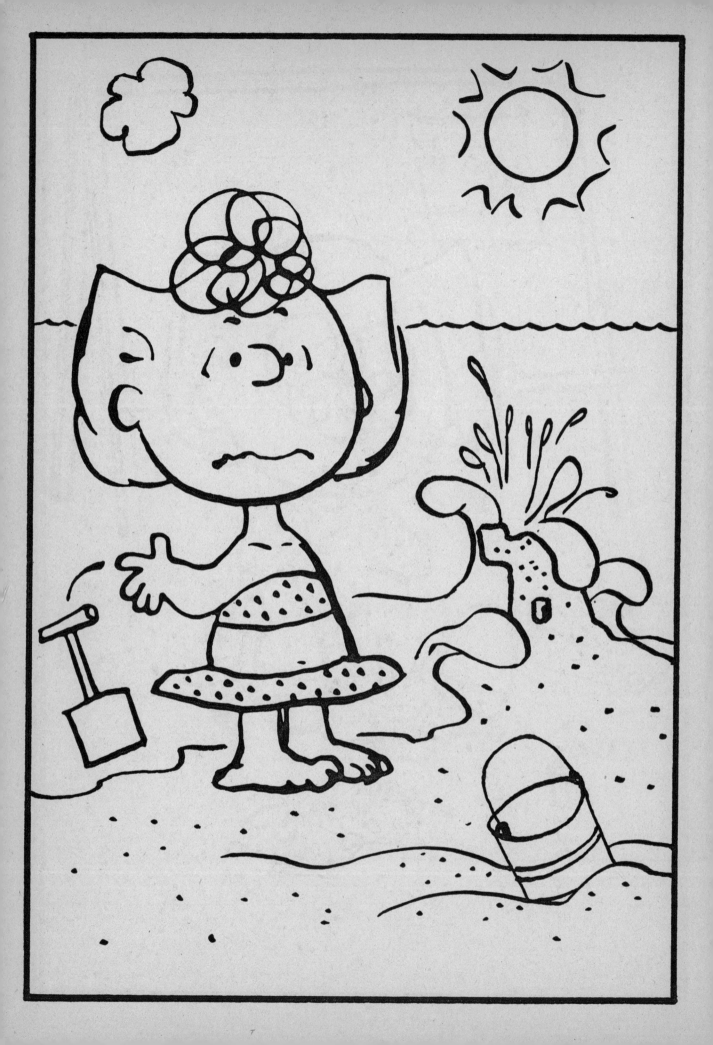

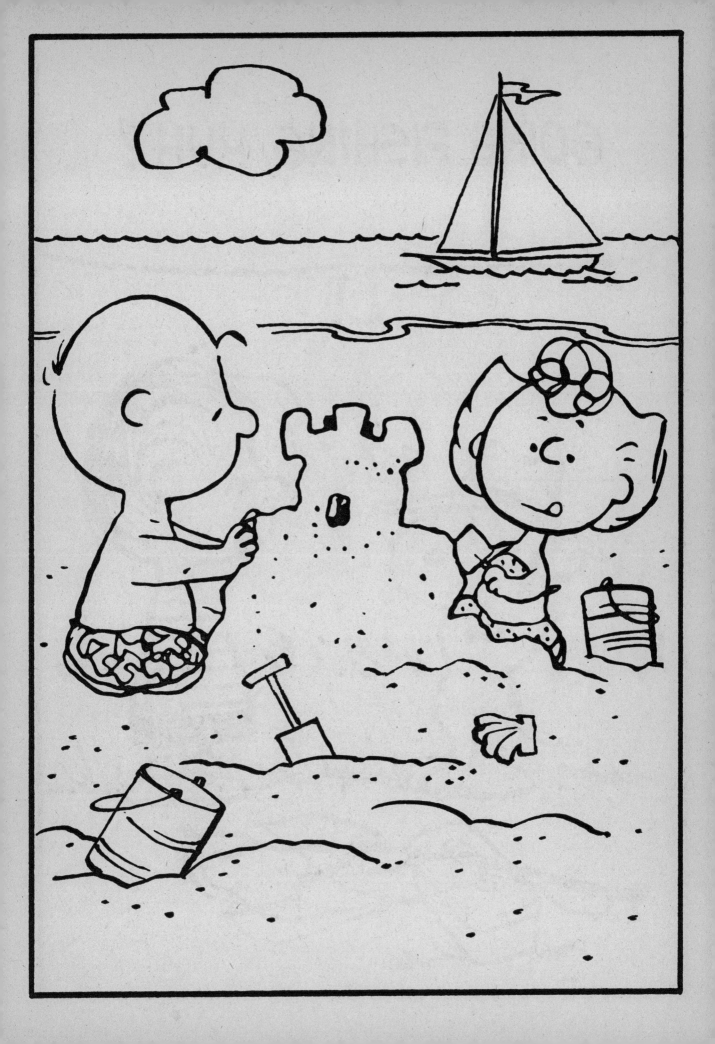

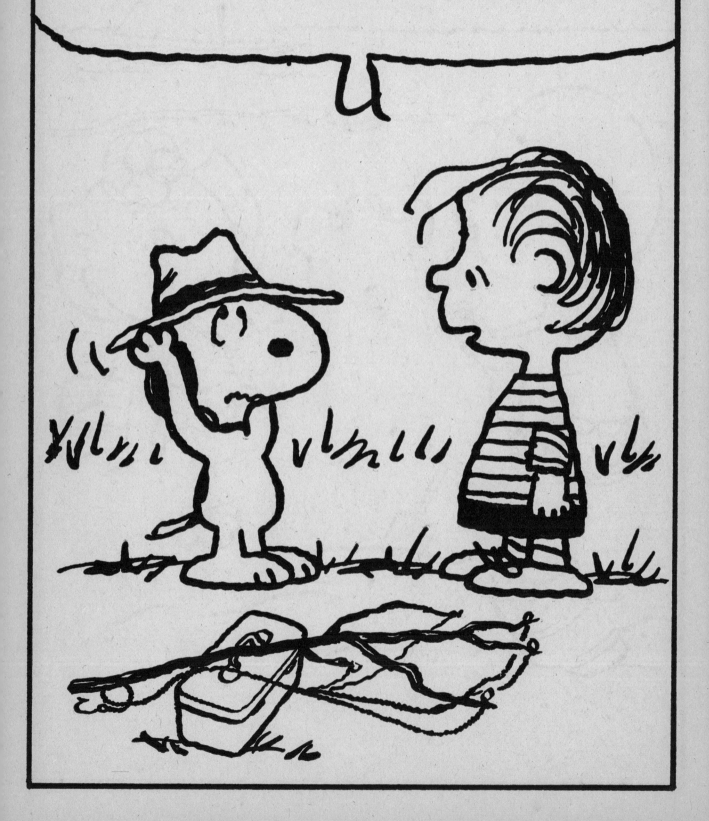

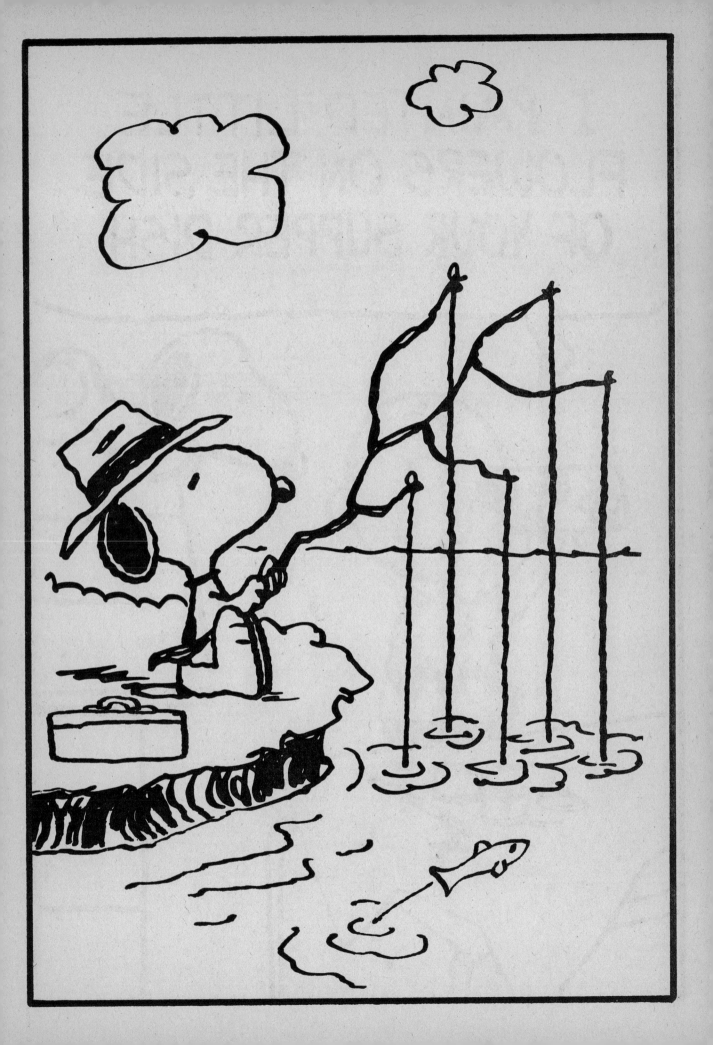

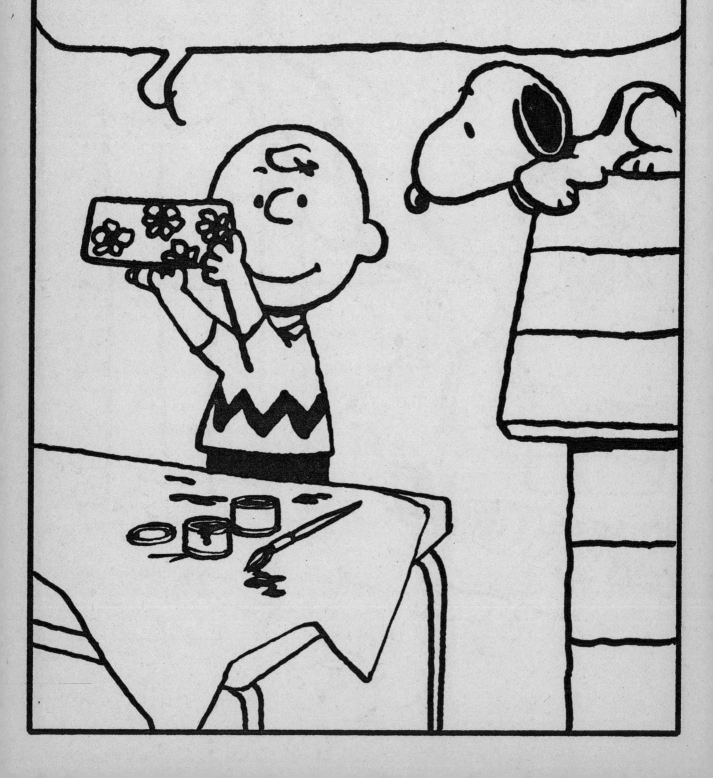

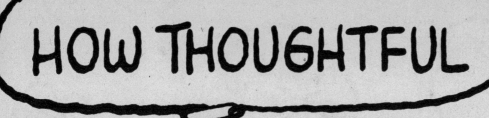
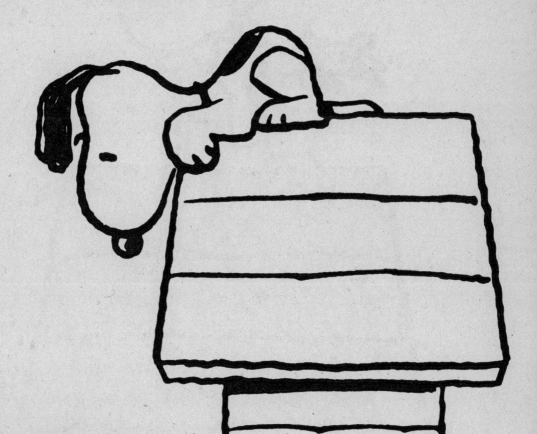
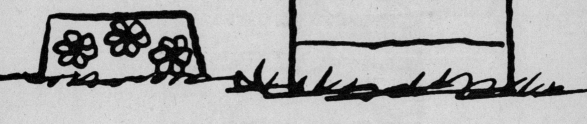

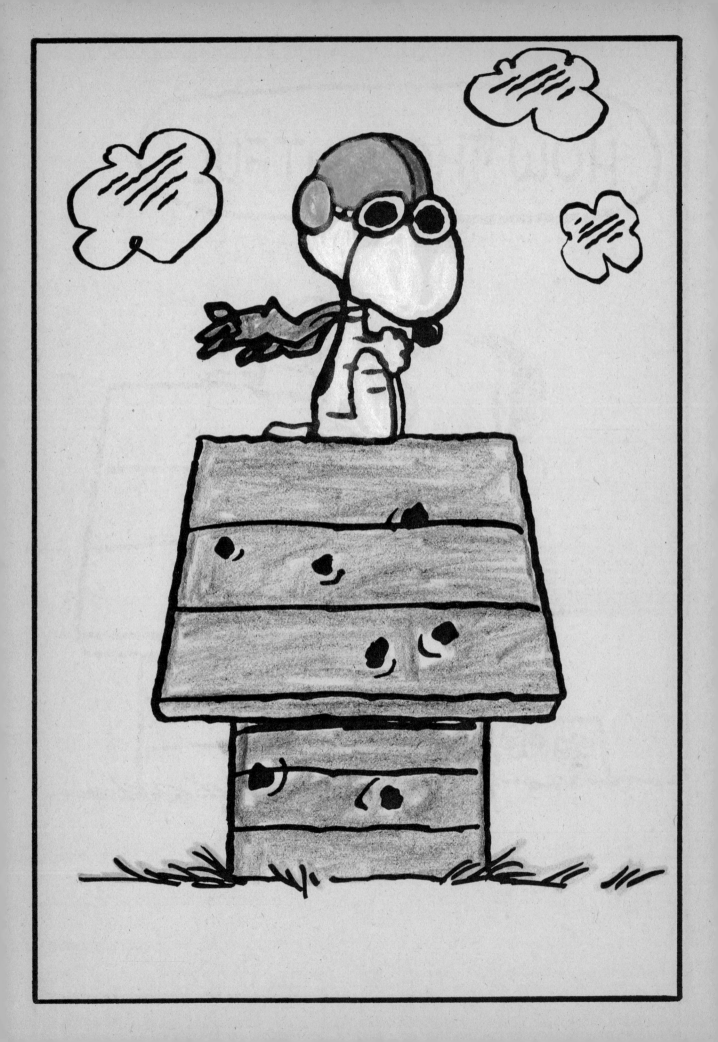

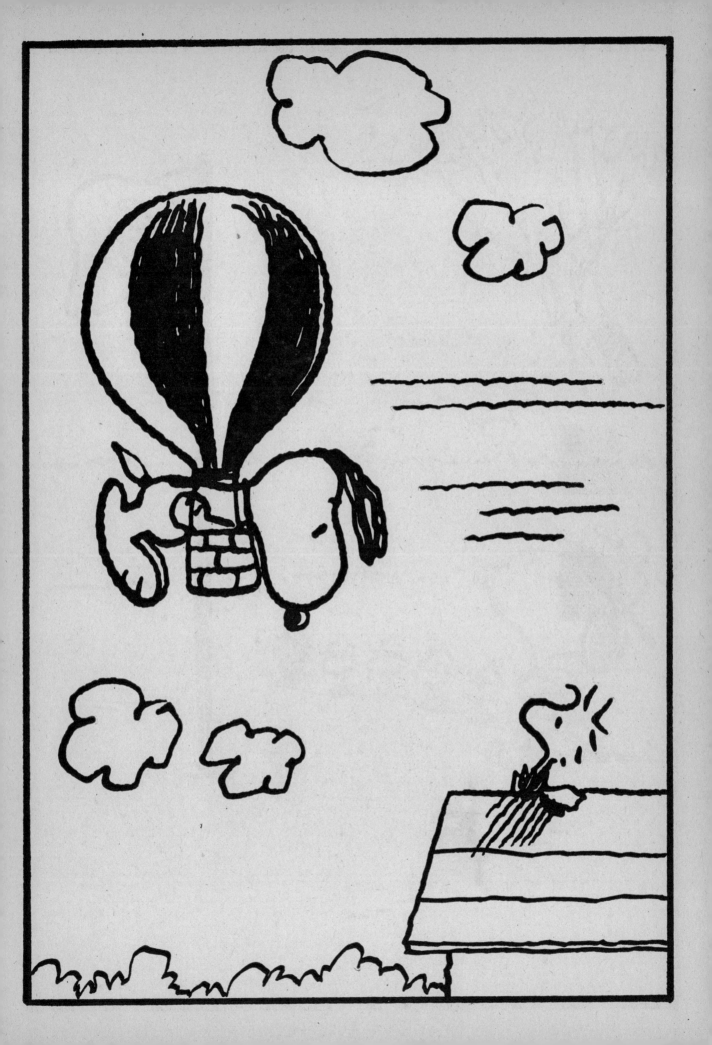

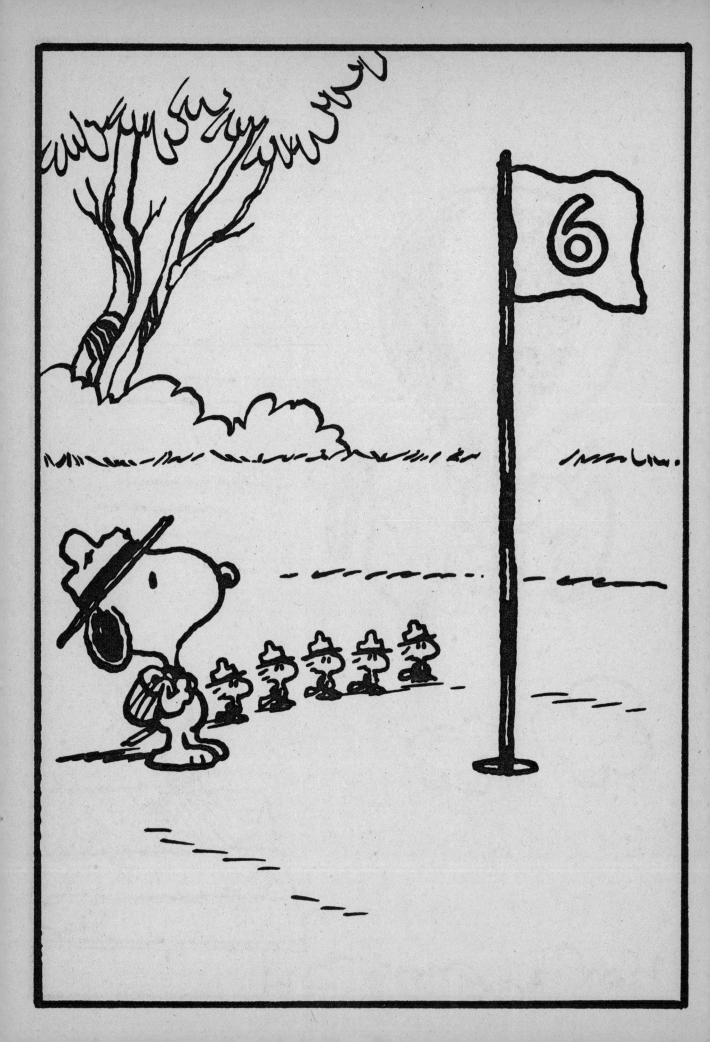

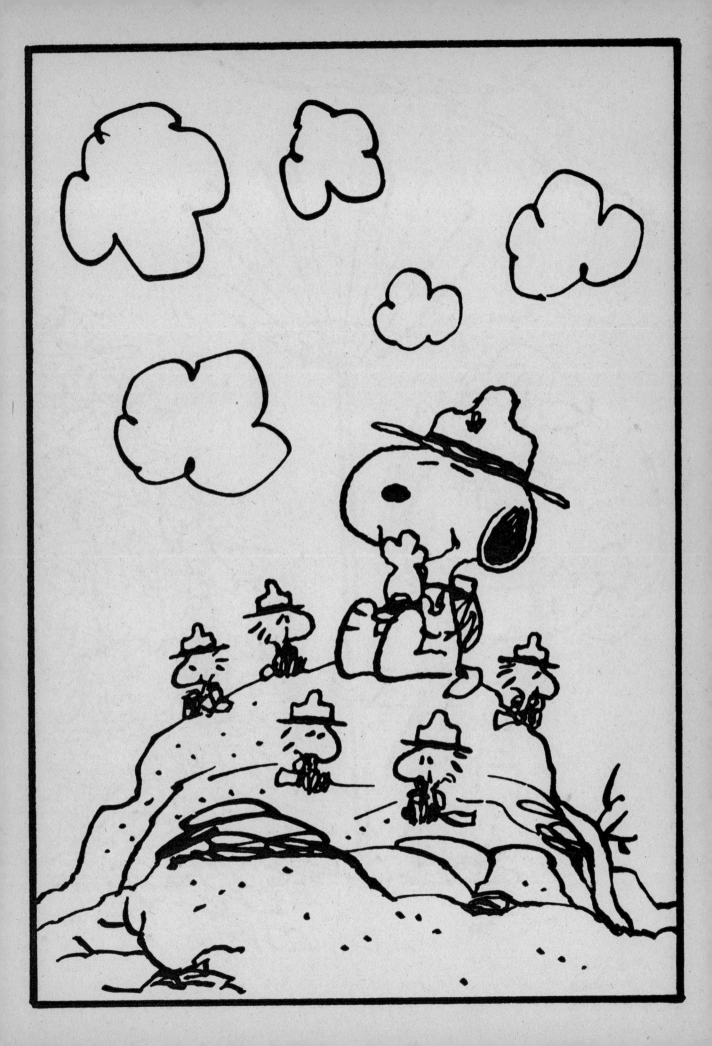

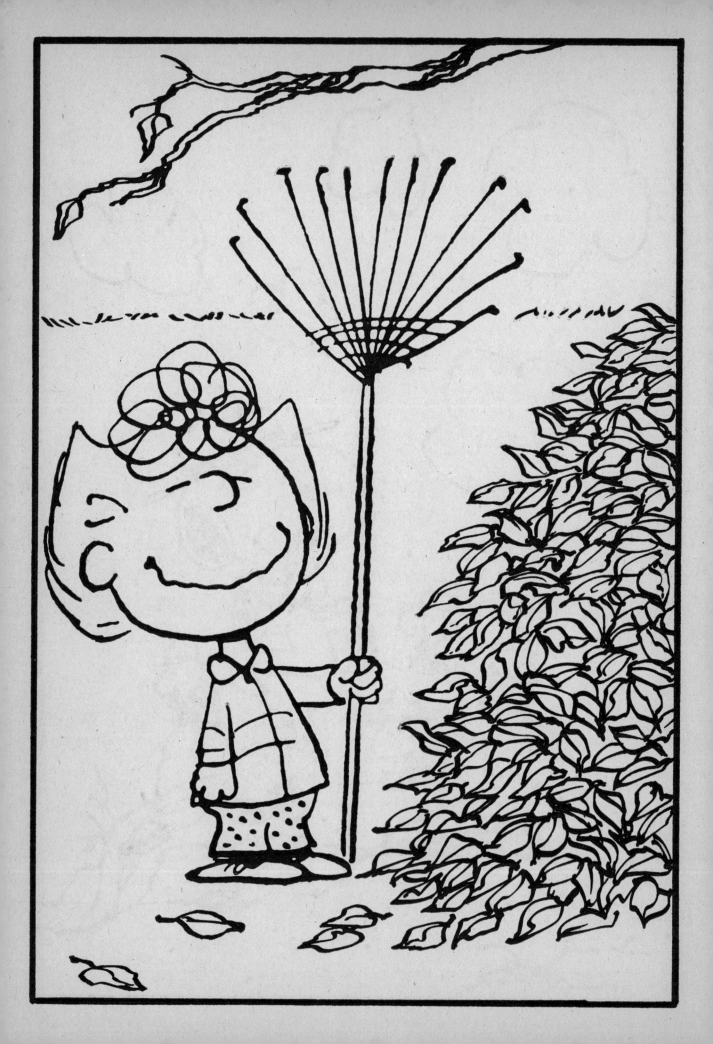

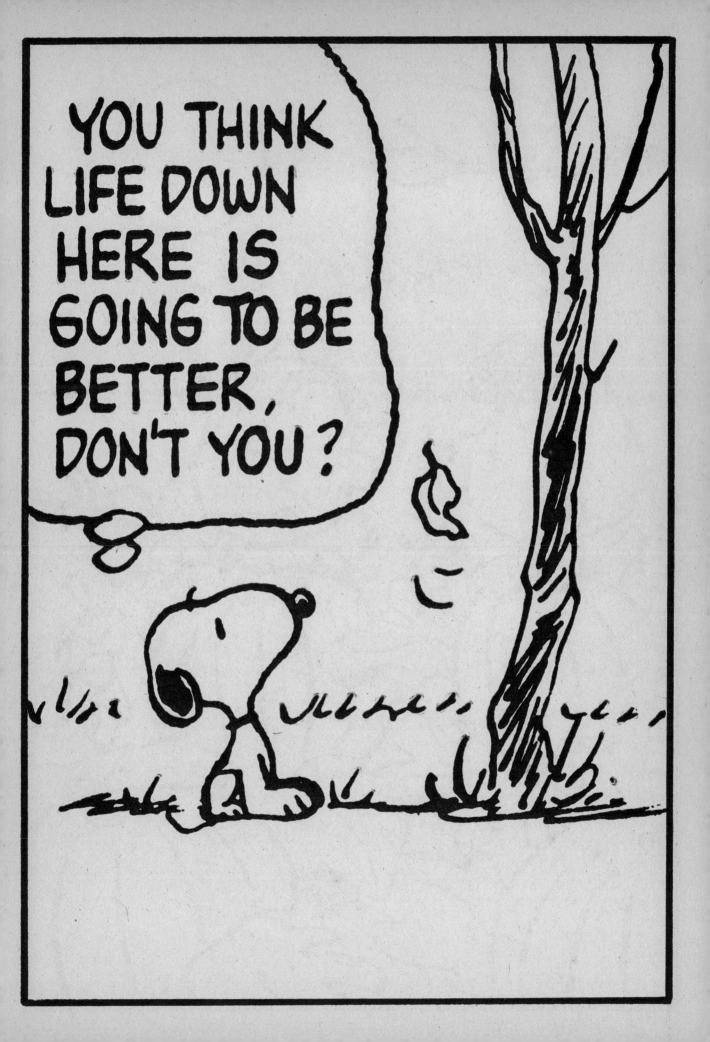

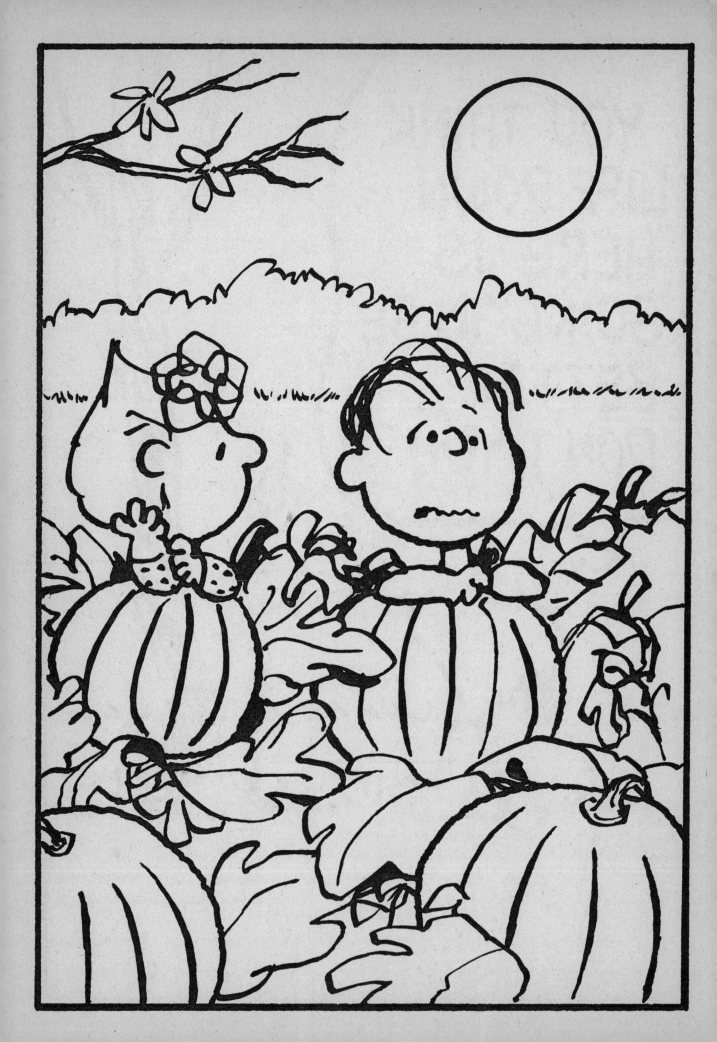

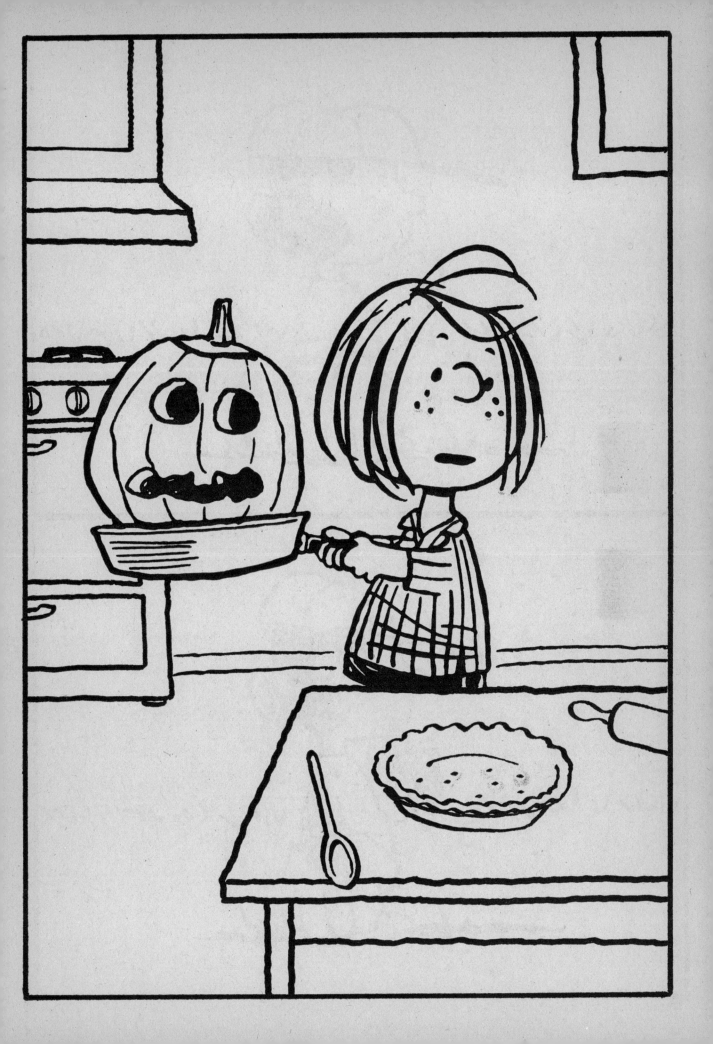

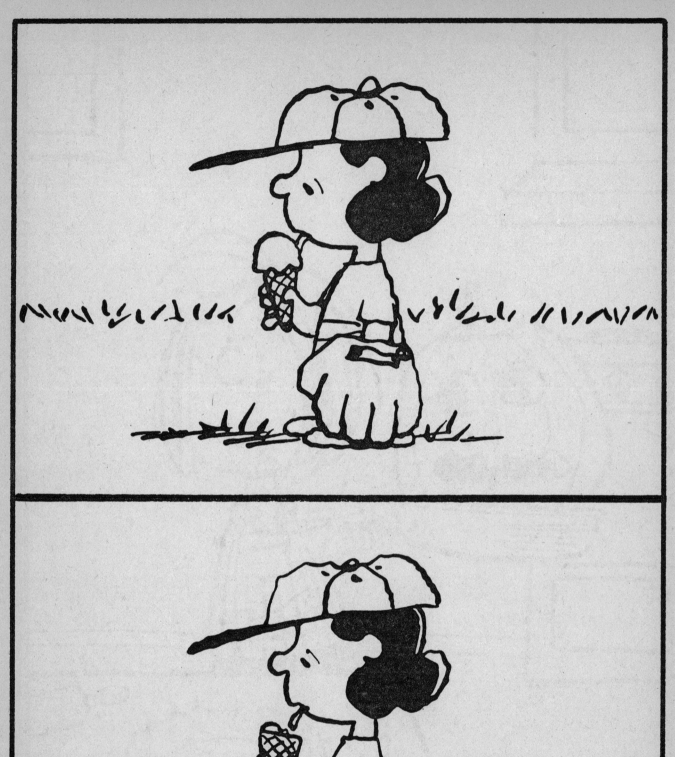
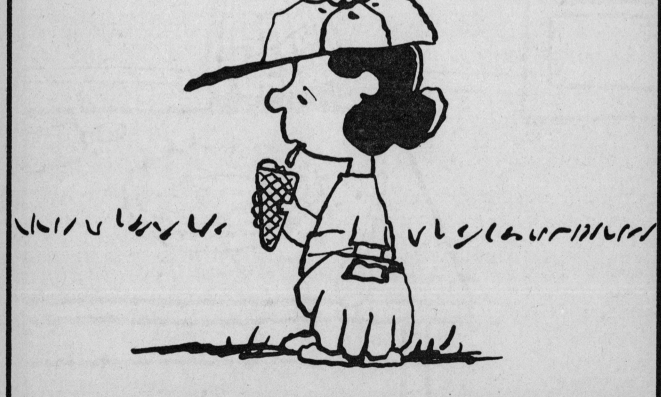

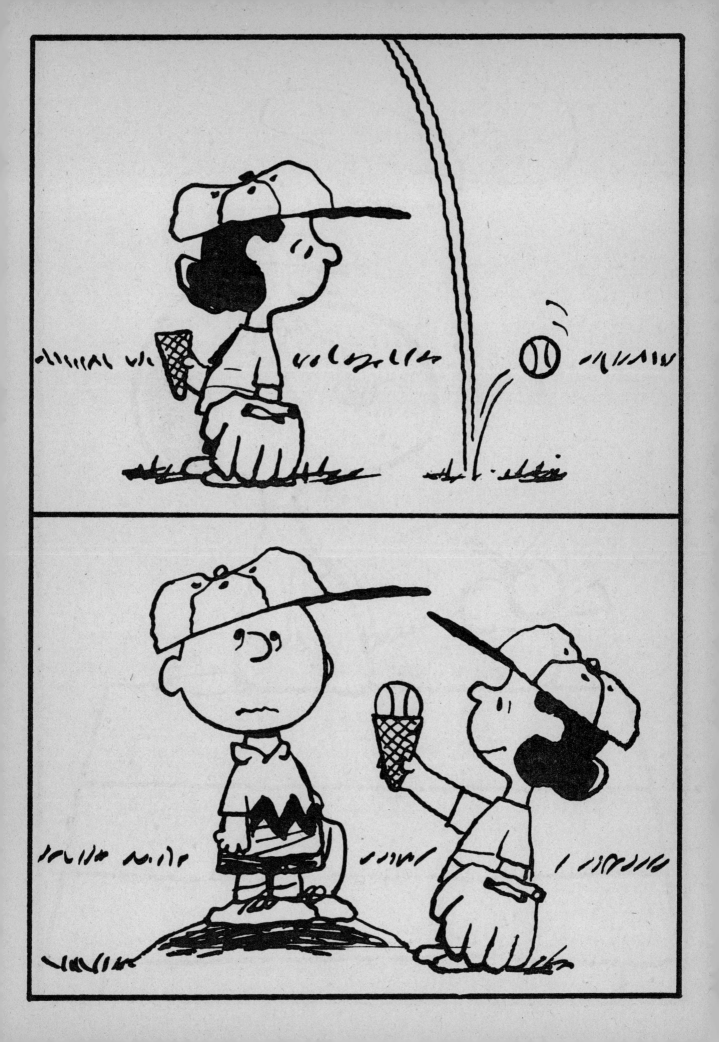

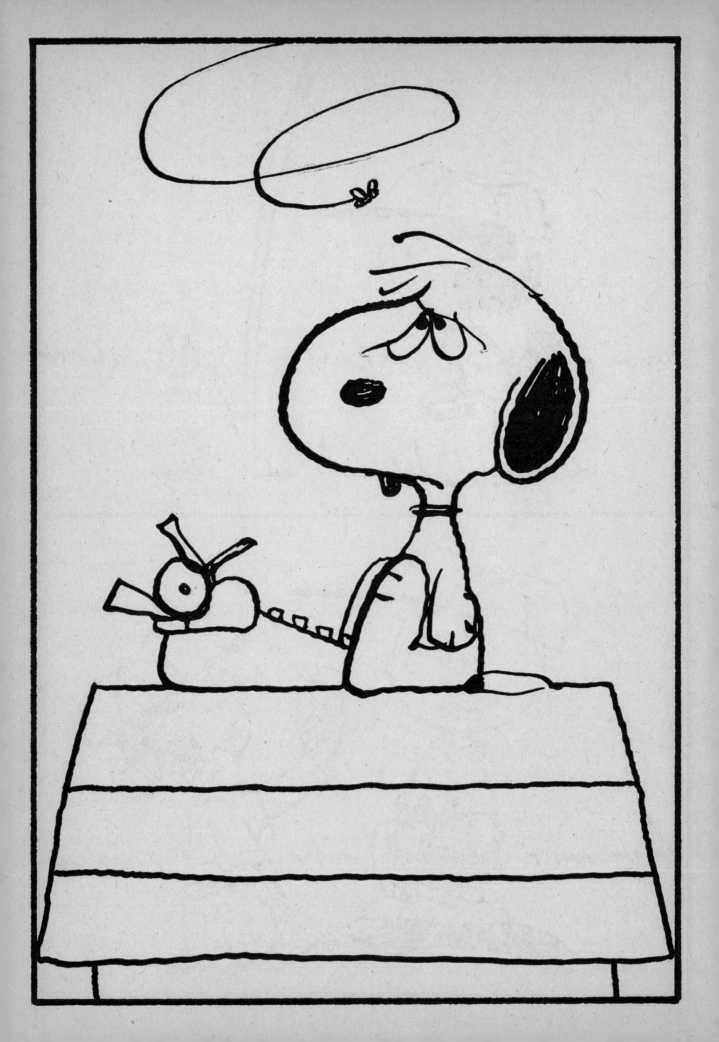

a teeny tiny little yellow bird.

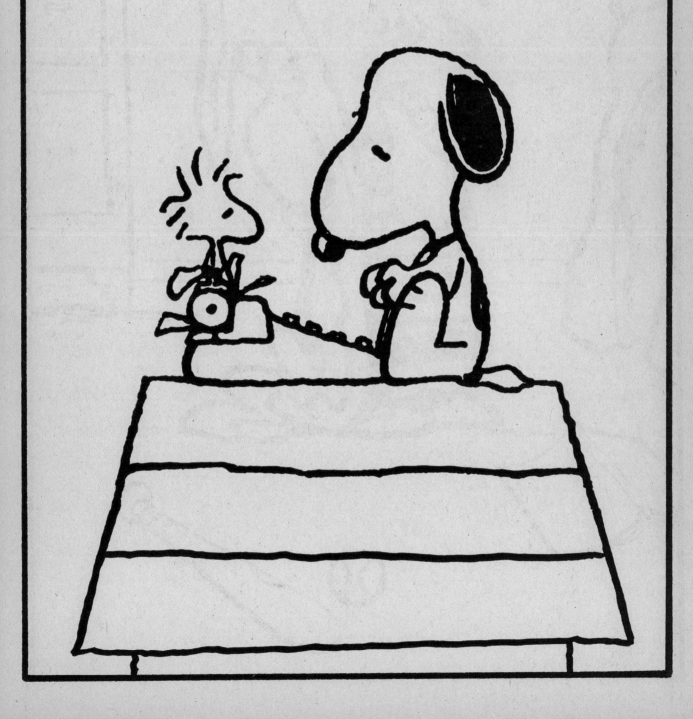

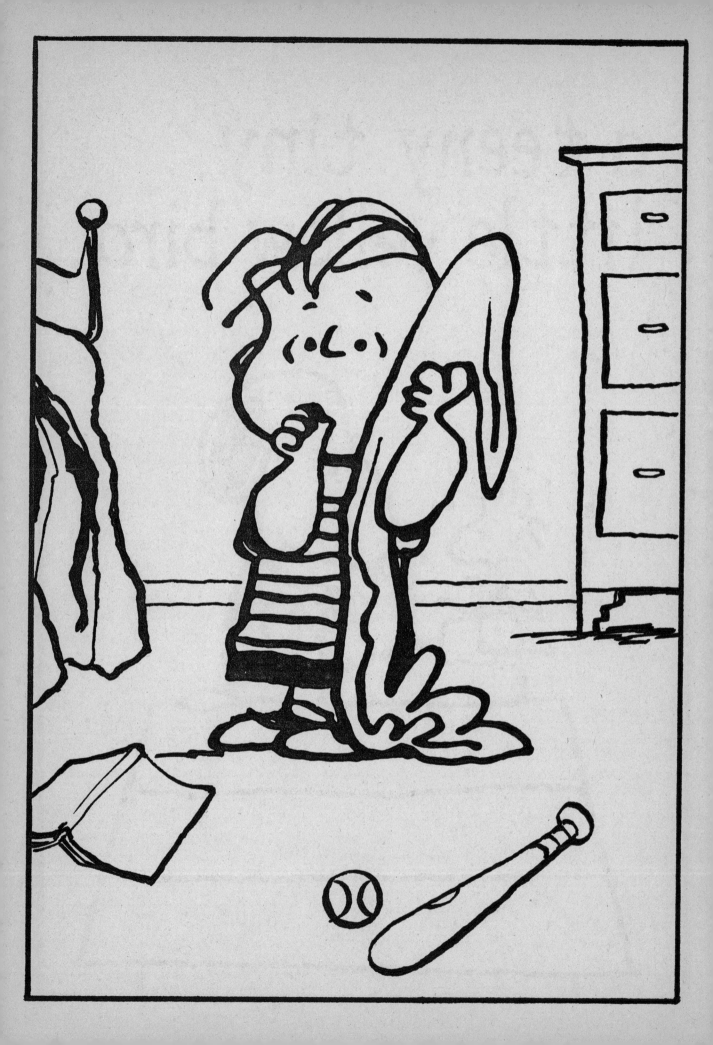

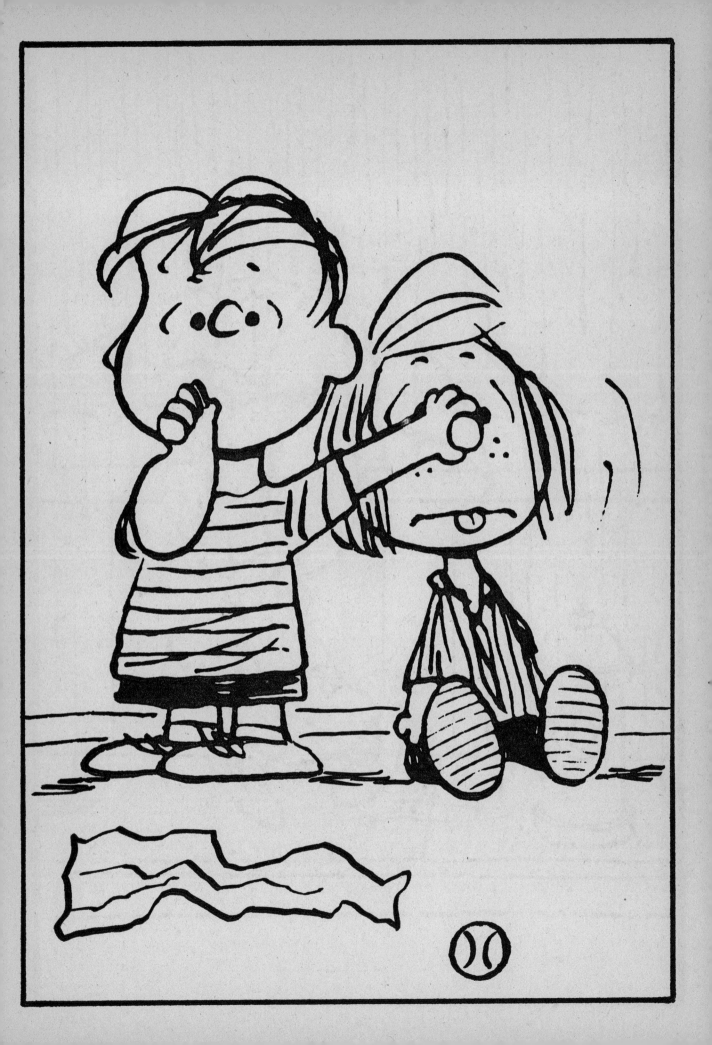

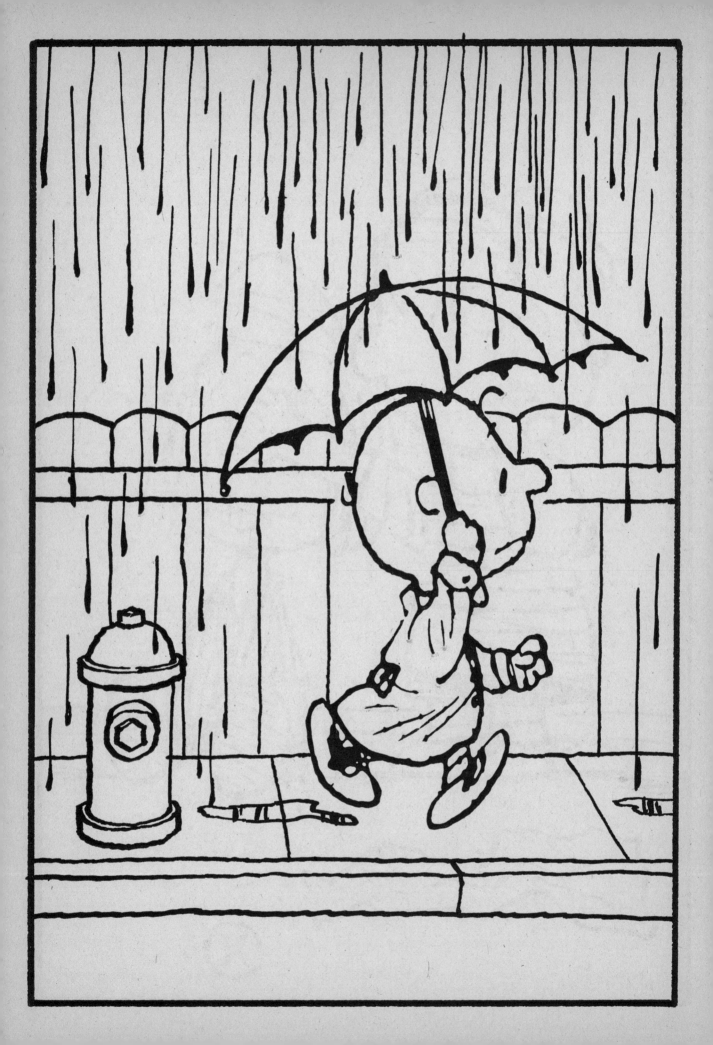

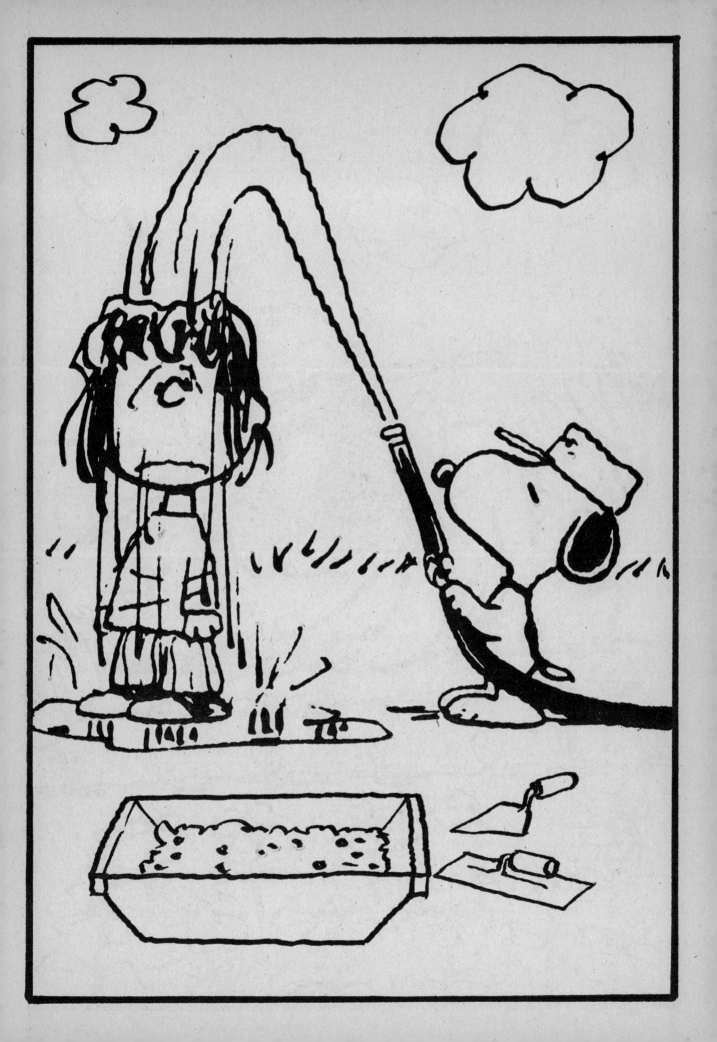

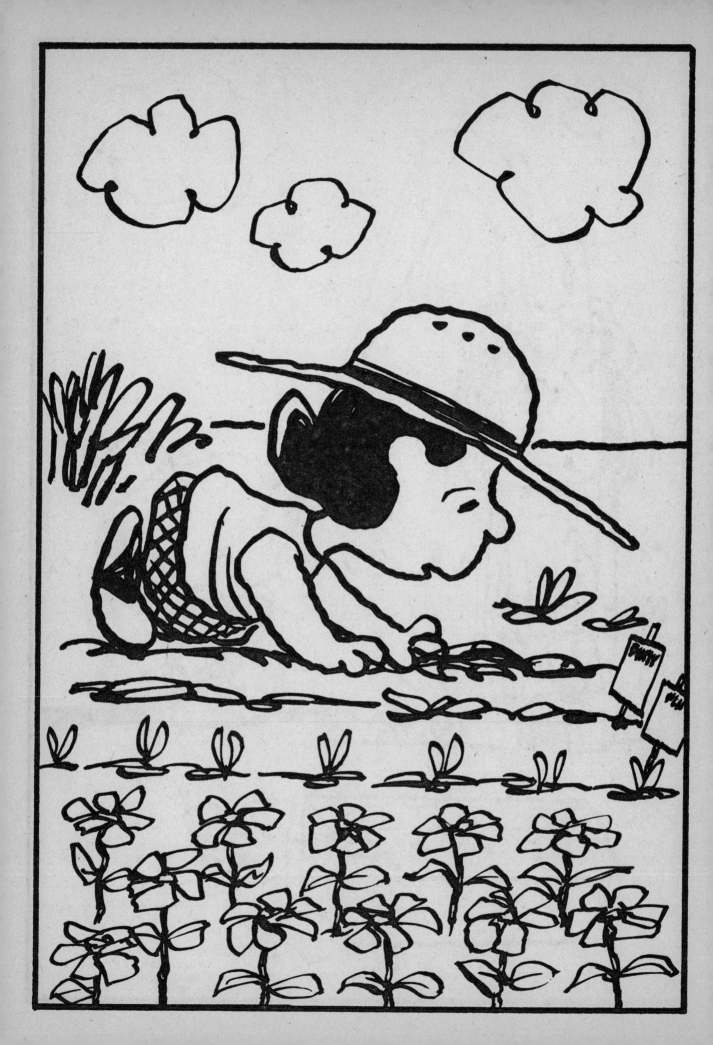

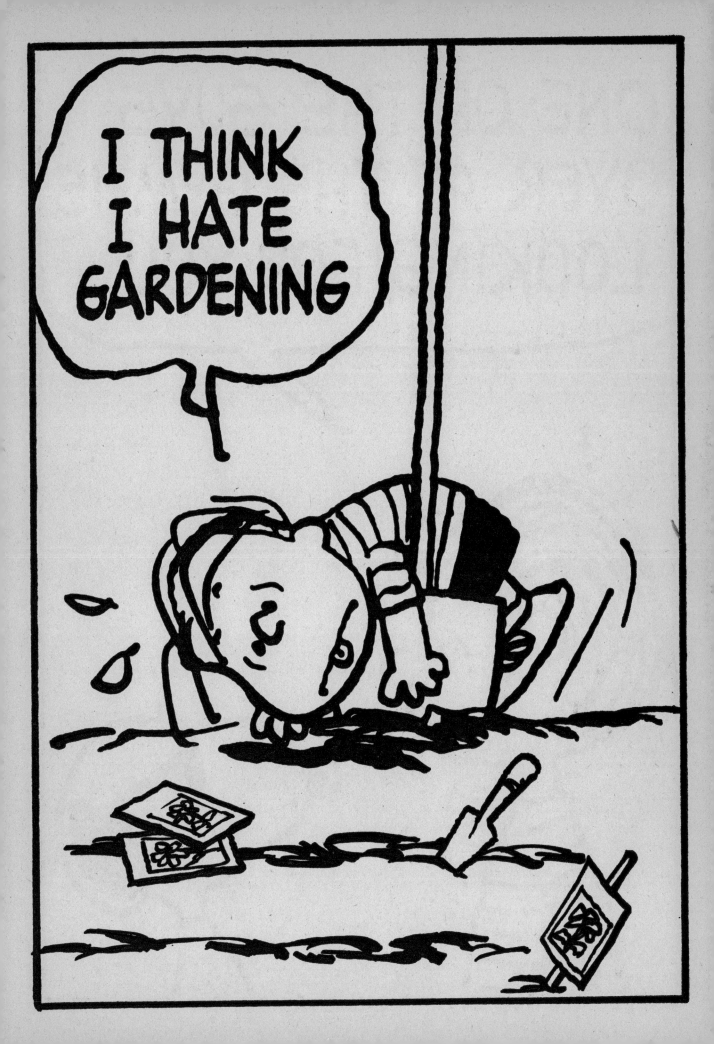

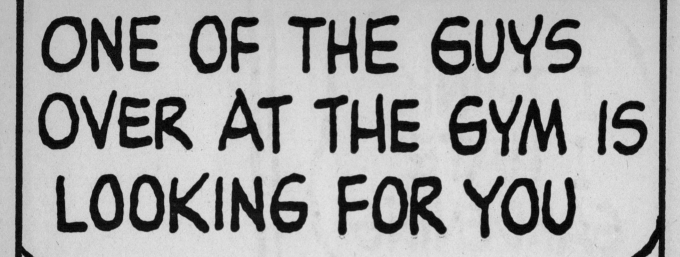
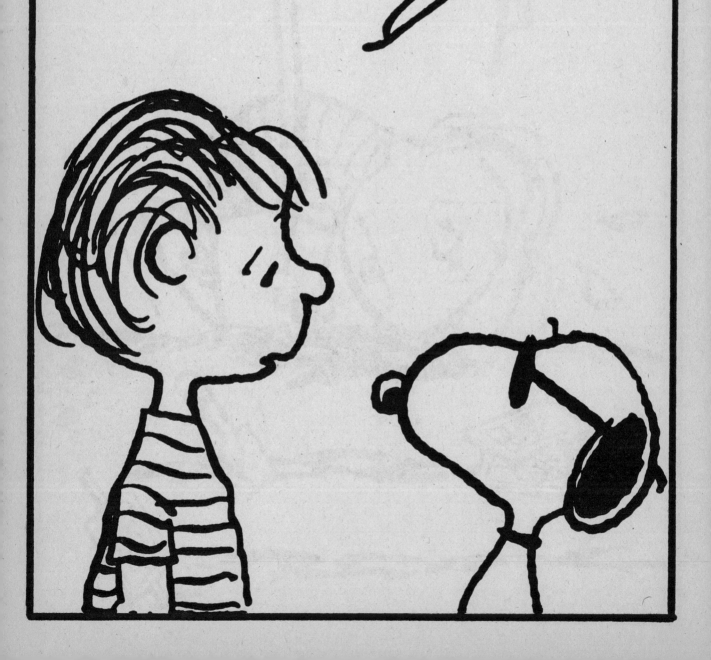

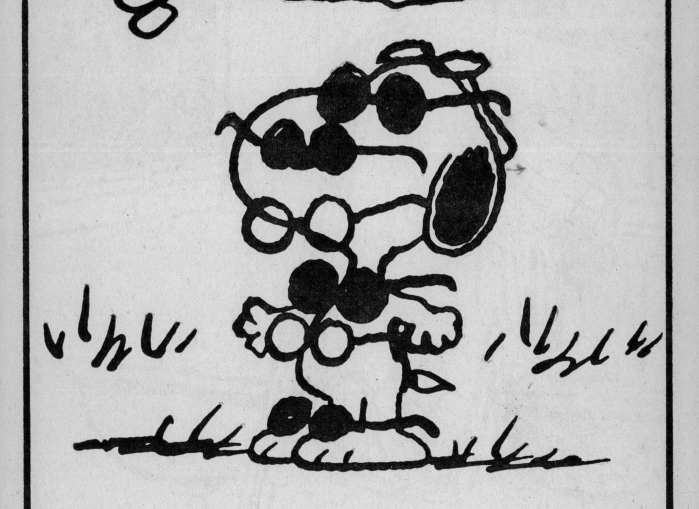

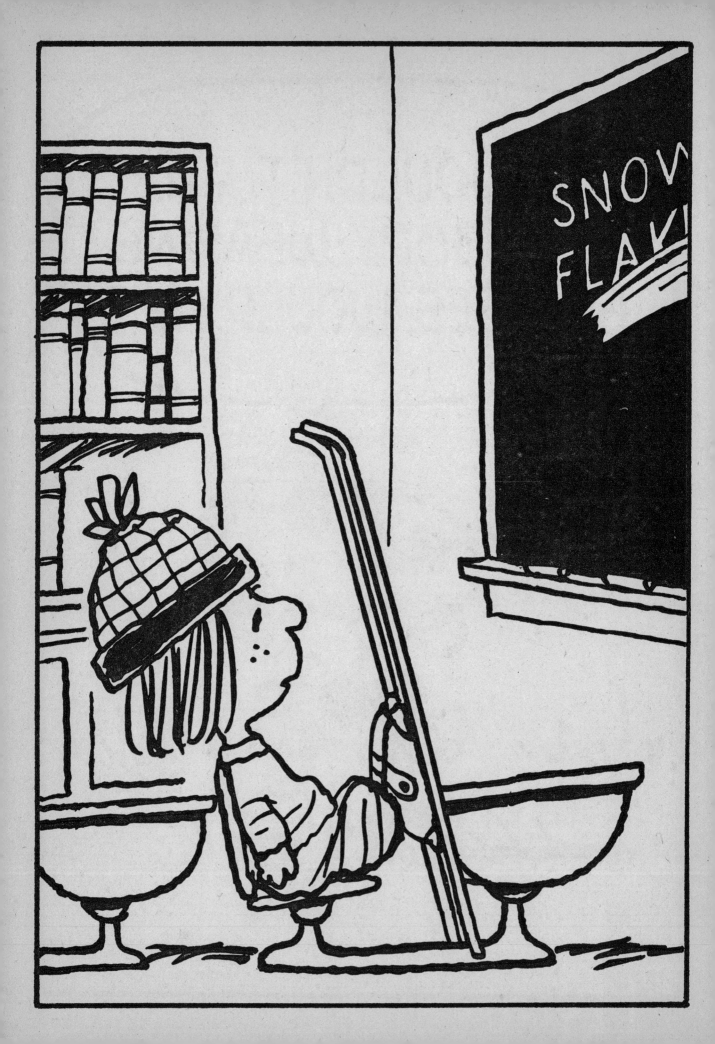

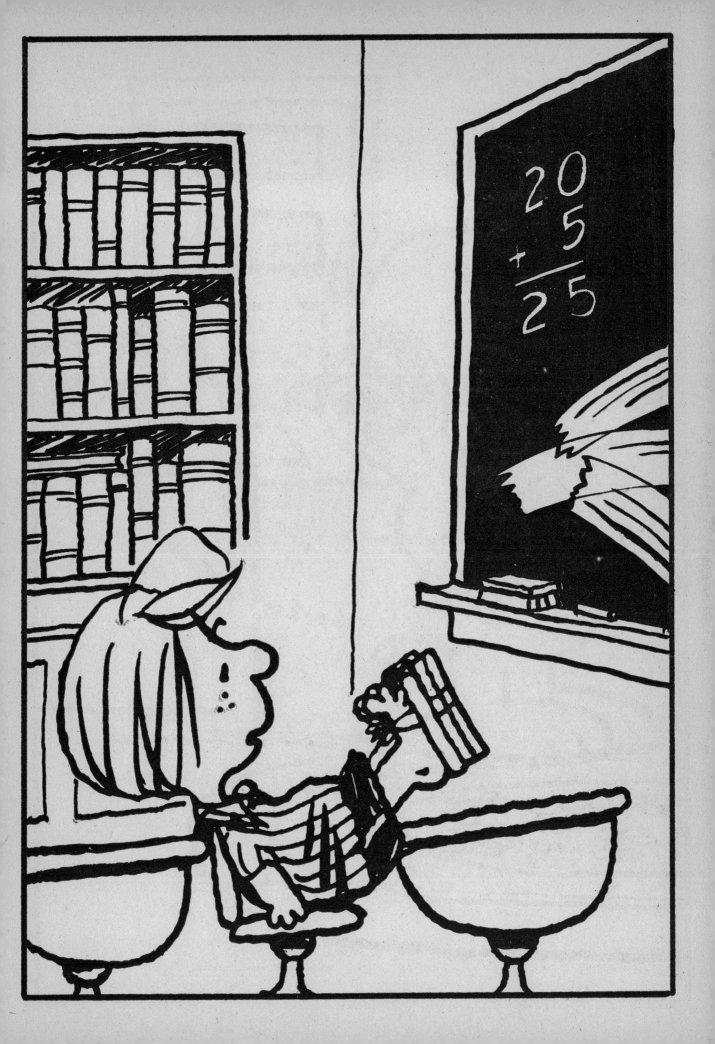

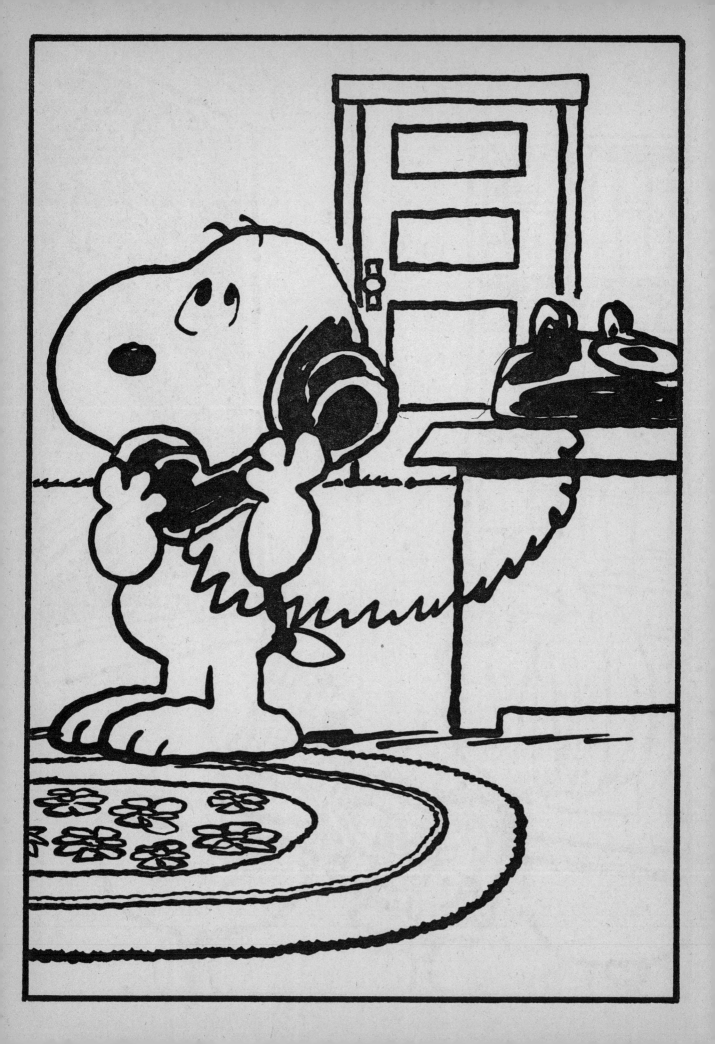

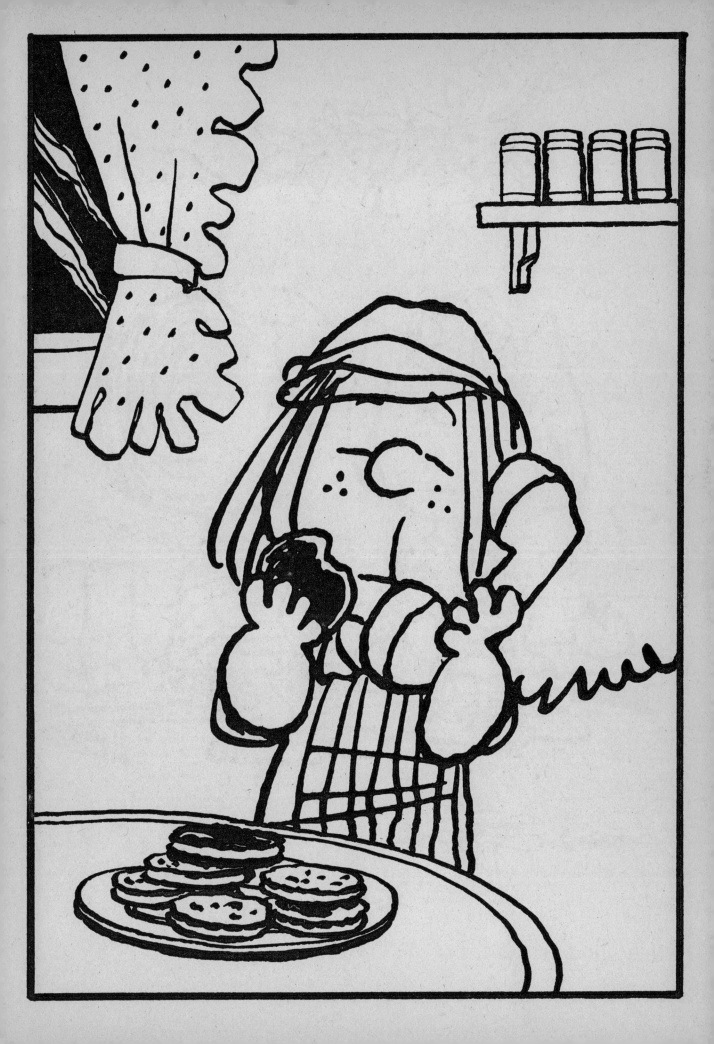

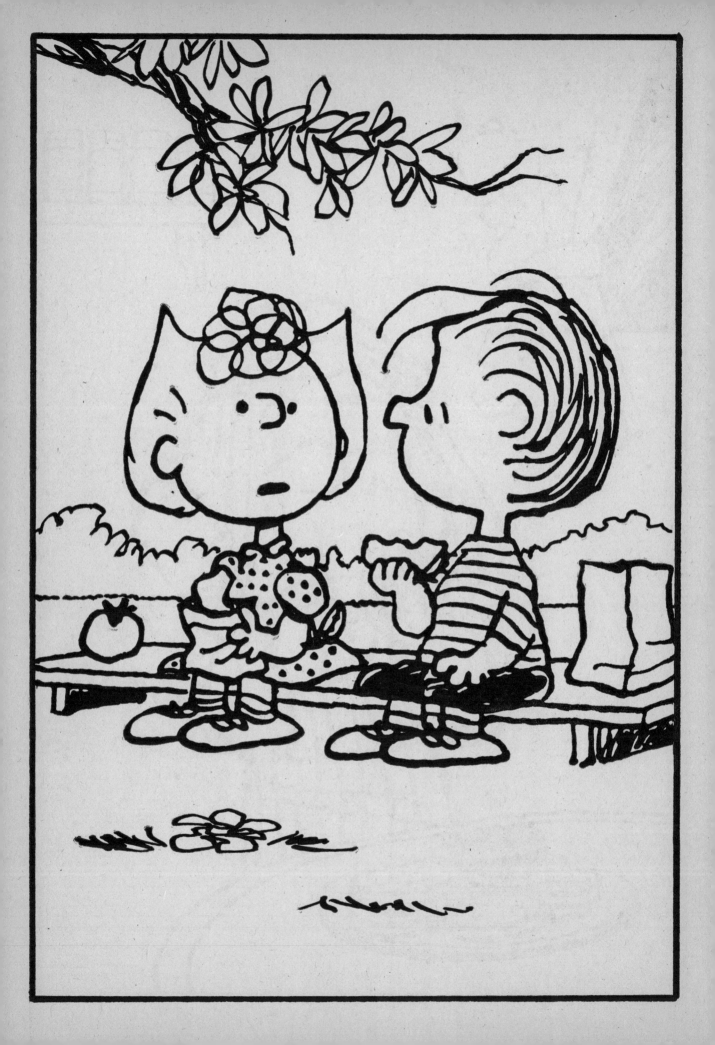

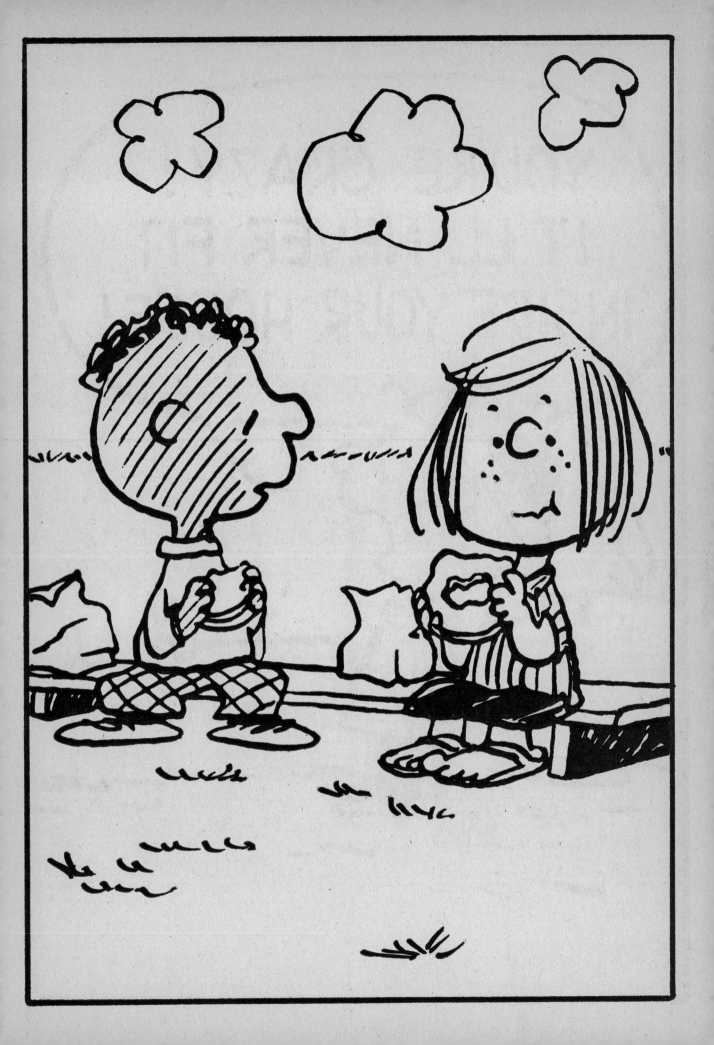

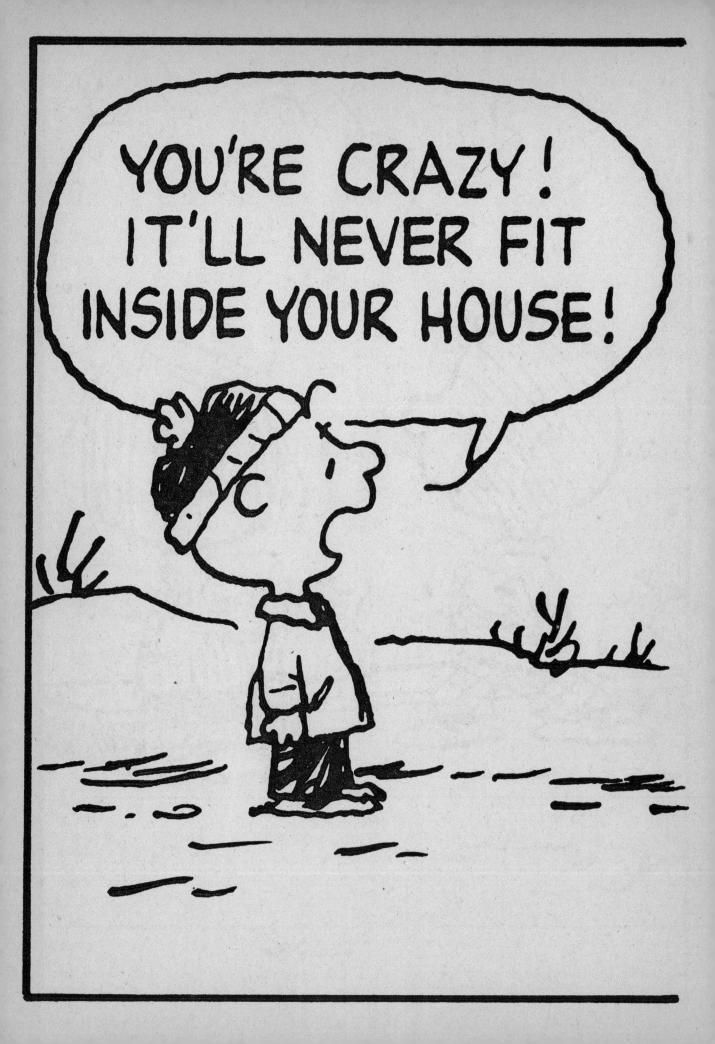

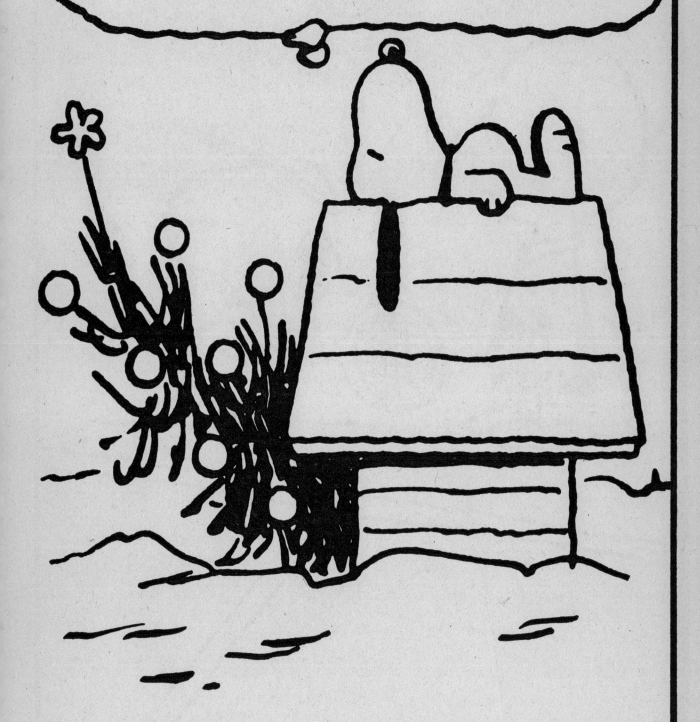

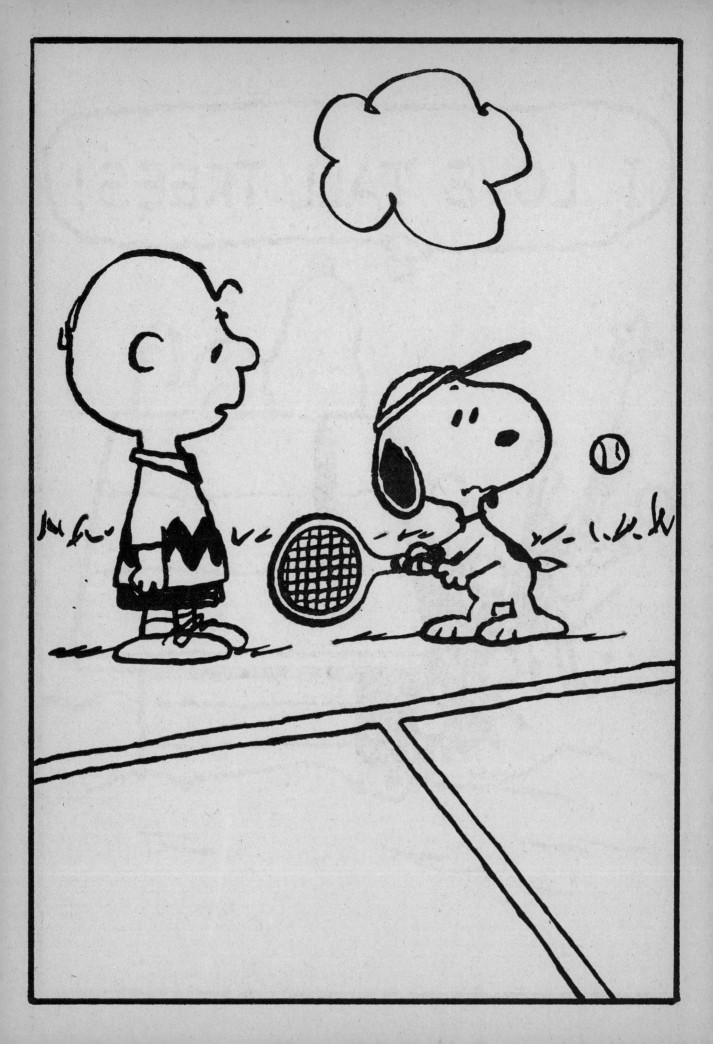

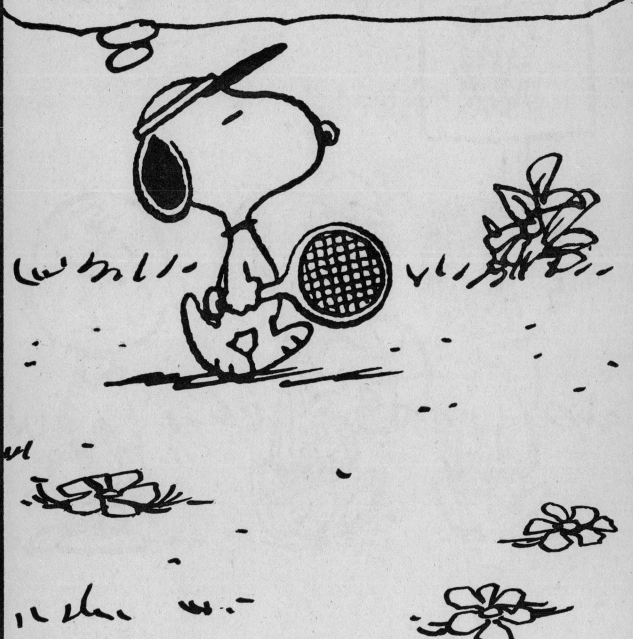

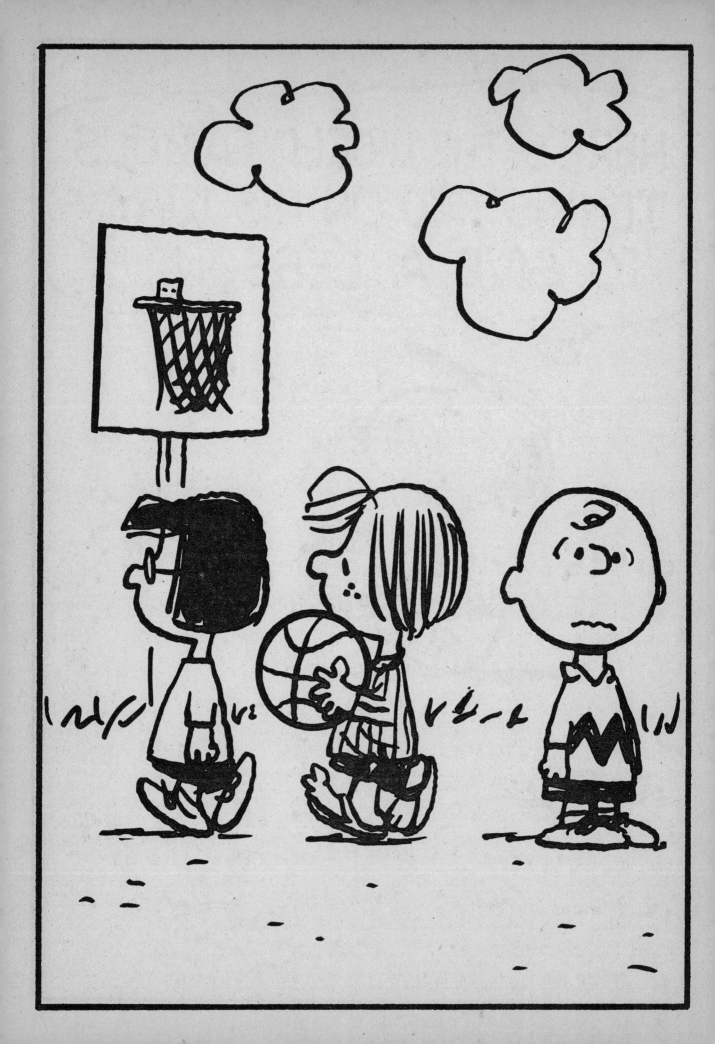

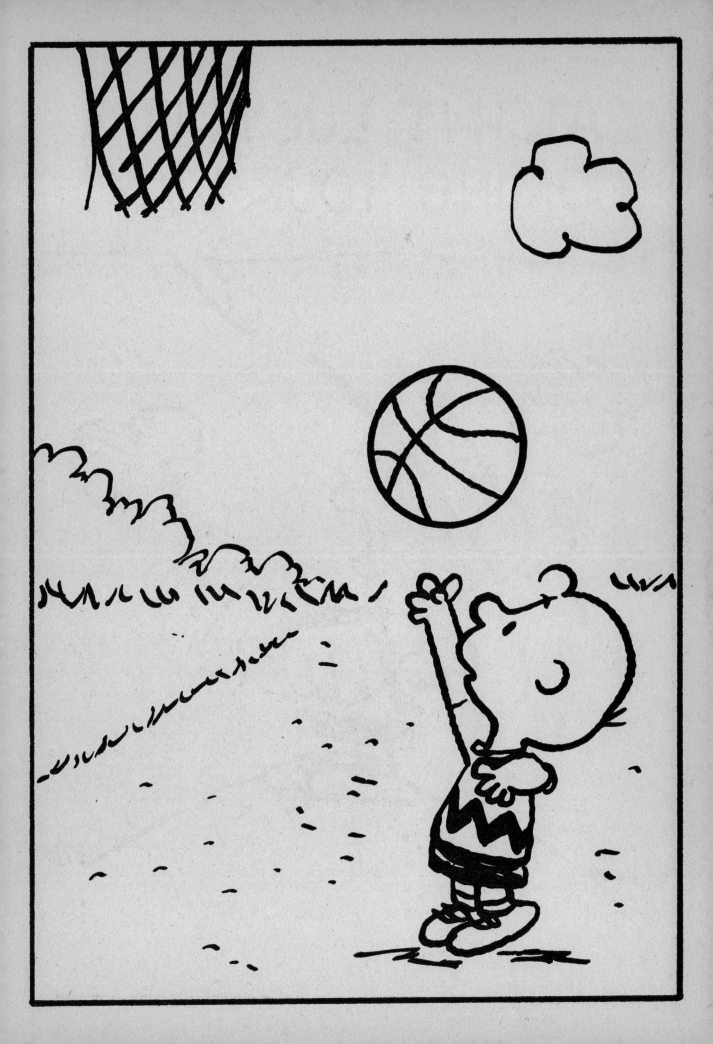

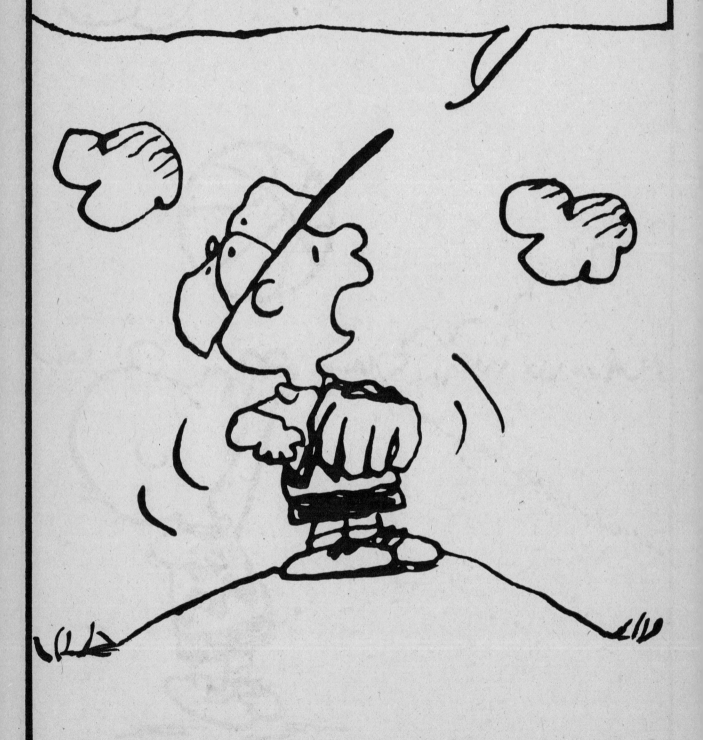

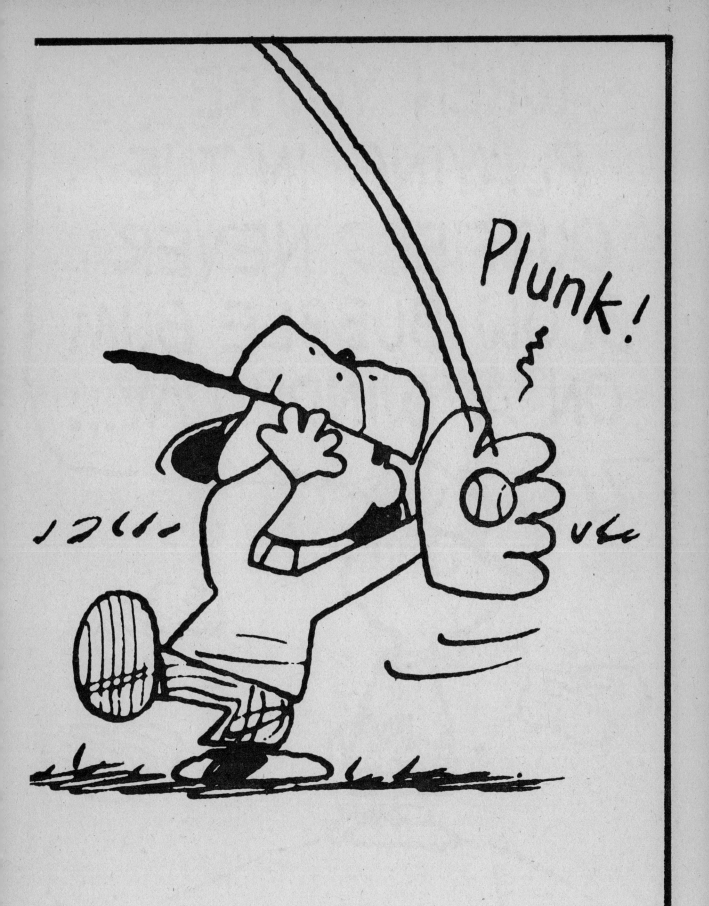

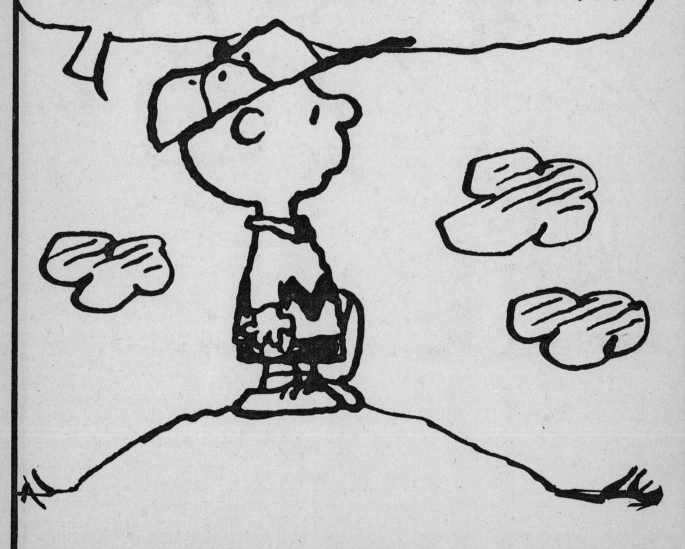

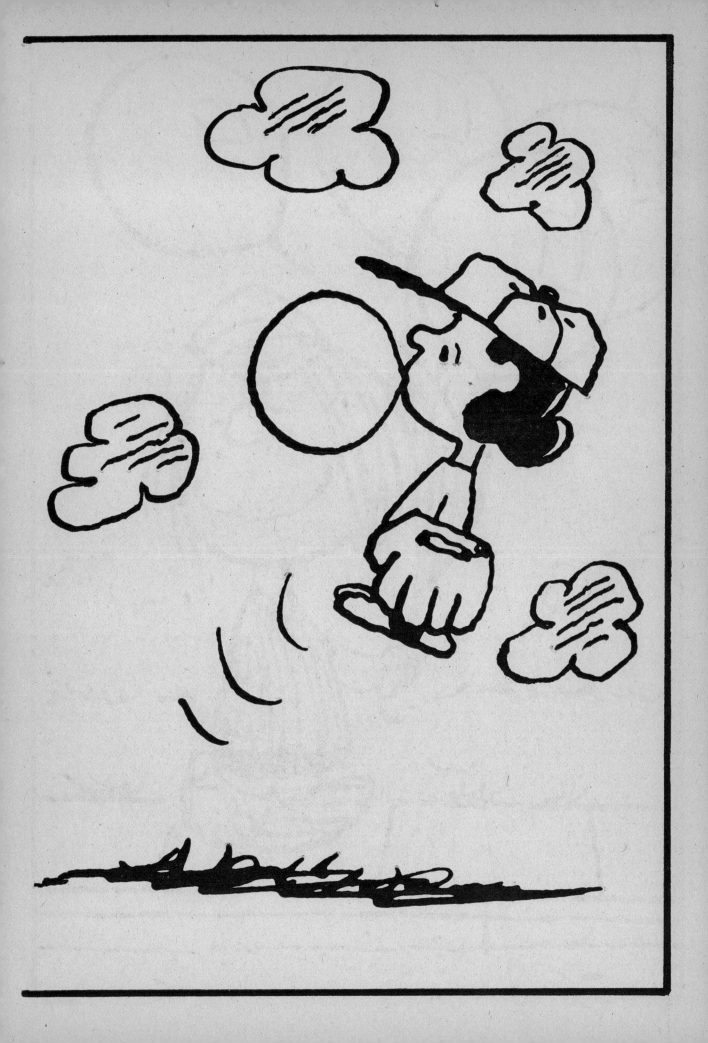

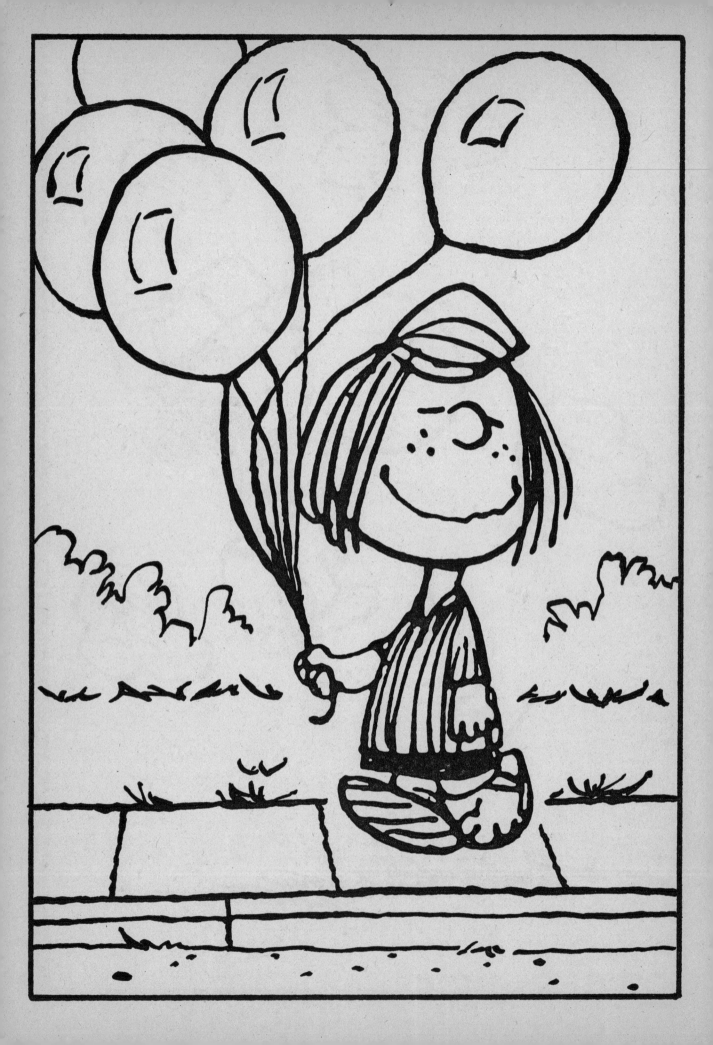

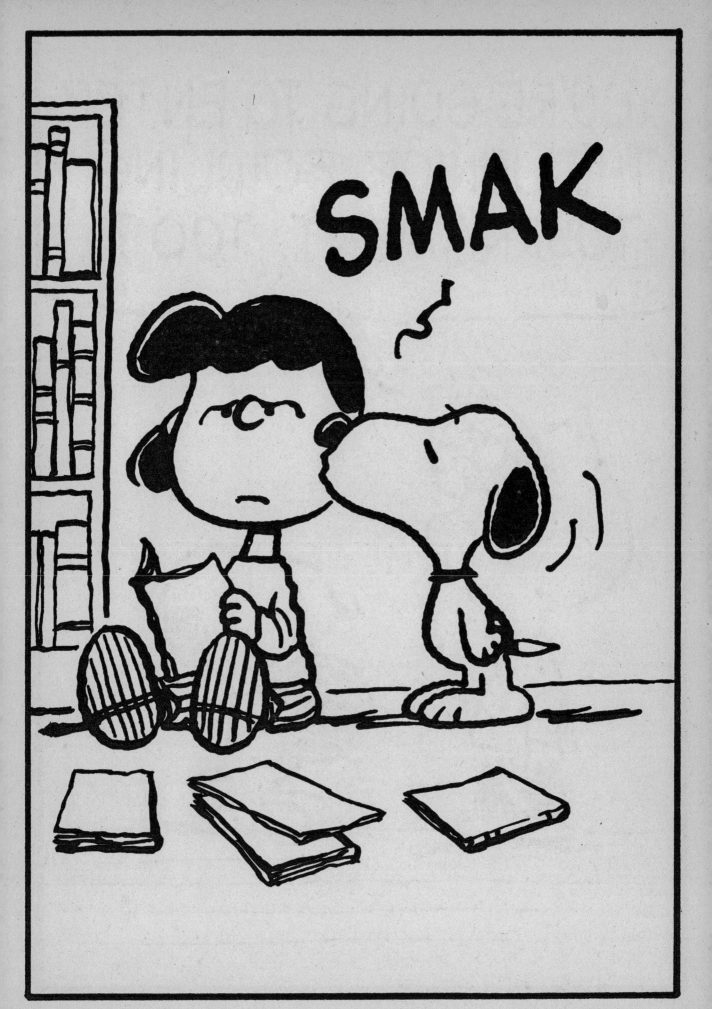

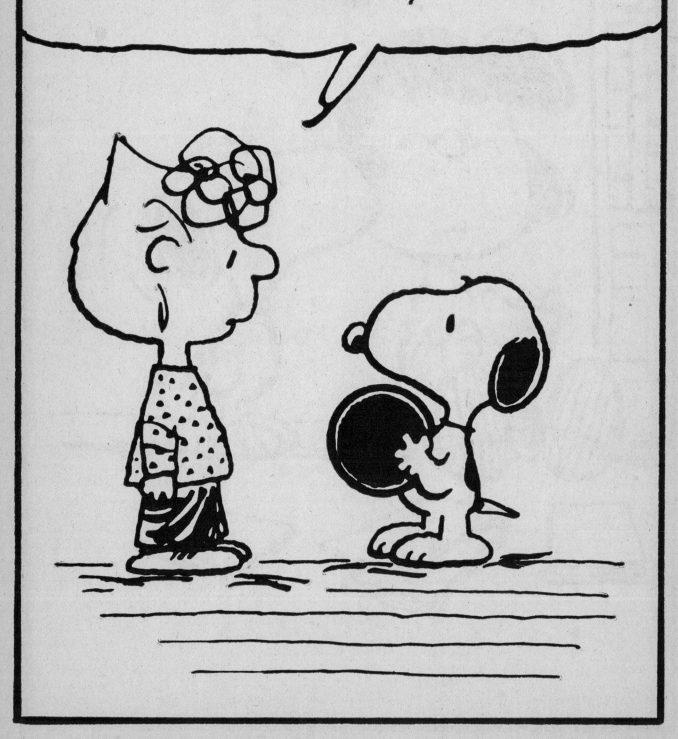

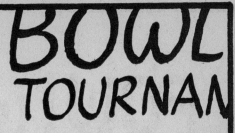

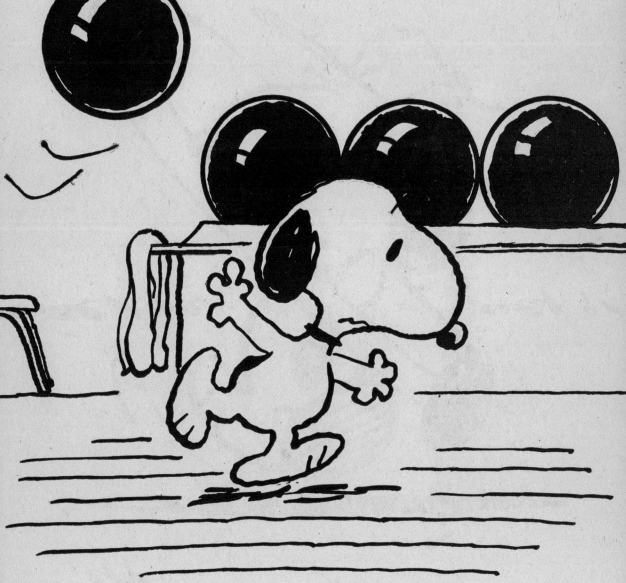

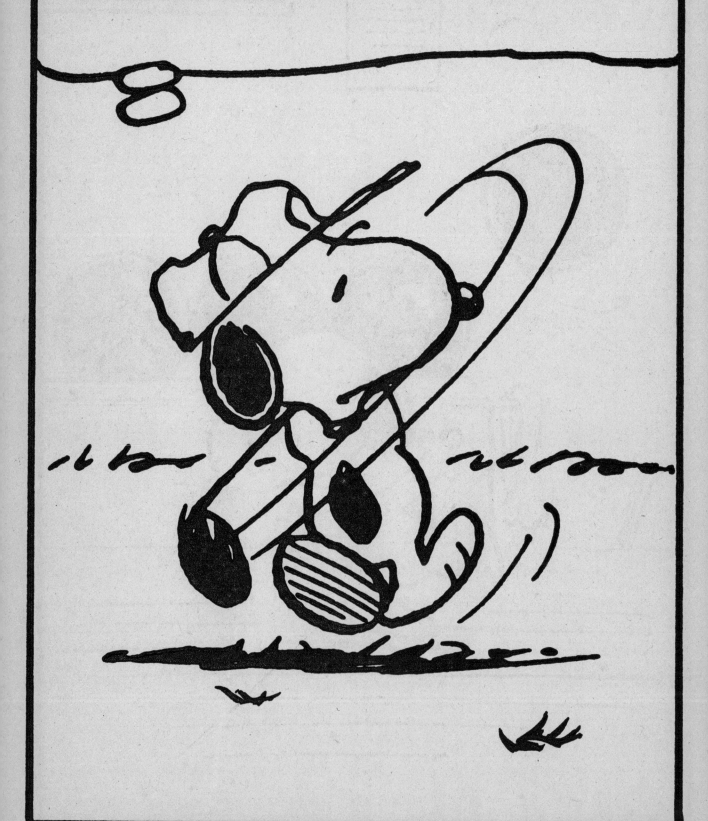

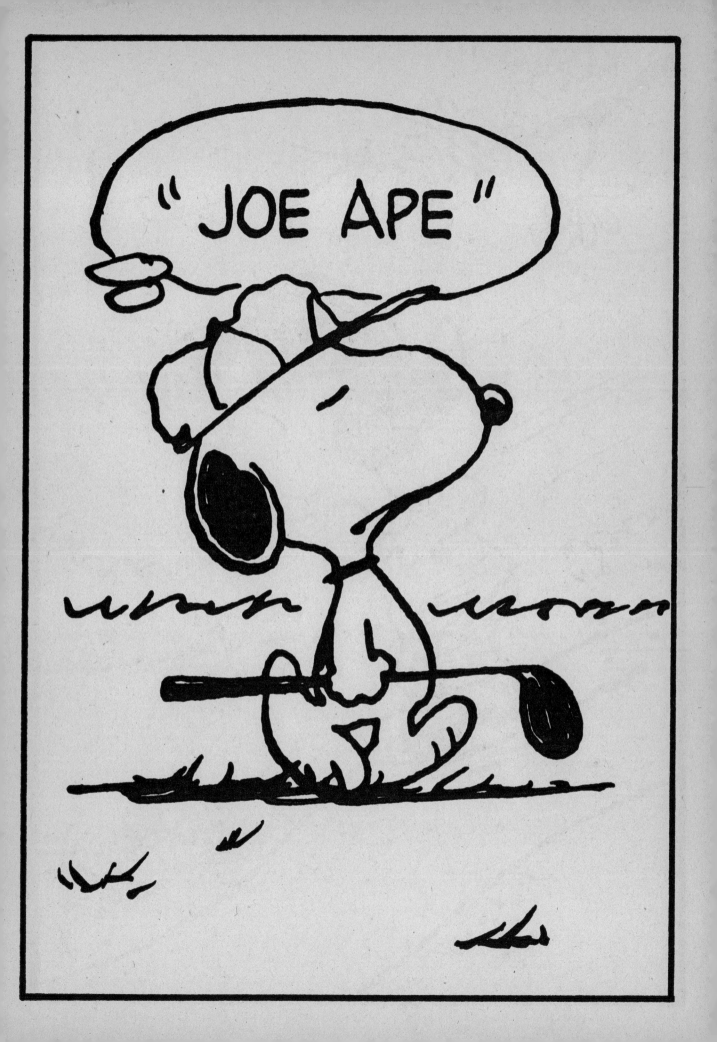

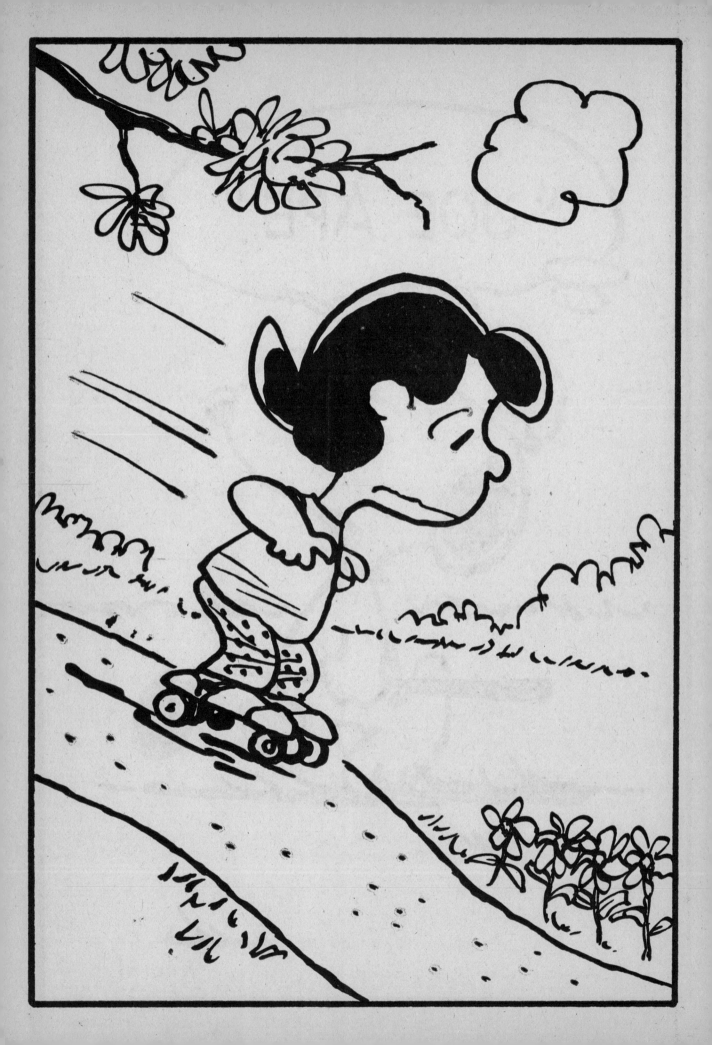